CW00808498

Cloud Gazing

by Michael James

HATS
OFF™

Cloud Gazing

Copyright © 2003 Michael James
All rights reserved.

No part of this book may be reproduced or
retransmitted in any form or by any means without the
written permission of the publisher.

Published by Hats Off Books™
610 East Delano Street, Suite 104
Tucson, Arizona 85705, U.S.A.
www.hatsoffbooks.com

ISBN: 1-58736-231-7 (hardcover)
ISBN: 1-58736-192-2 (paperback)
LCCN: 2003091848

Cover art by Michael James
Book design by Atilla L. Vékony

This book is for Robert and Jean

Prologue

I met the devil once. There is, I suppose, no scientific way to prove this to anybody apart from myself, but it remains a fact. I met the devil on the day that the summer died.

Perhaps this is a poor description—perhaps the summer does not die, is not really an entity in itself. To many minds it is just a part of a natural cycle. But even so, there is always a day in September when the year suddenly grows too old to sustain its pretence at youth. After that time there may be sunny weather now and again, but the heart has gone out of it, there is the slightest of chills in the air, evening comes too soon and is not long and cool but brisk and cold. And, above all, there is the knowledge that the decline has a long way still to go. For if September is a man grown old, then it is a man who is old in comfort. He has enough strength for bursts of humour and gaiety. He is warm enough to please at times. But October is a different age. October has lost the will to even try, and the year tumbles ceaselessly towards winter. The rain extinguishes hopes, leaving a slushy dreariness that drifts unbroken toward the horizons of our dreams.

Then, that September day, when the summer is suddenly gone, is one that we feel most fully after the event. It is an event, but it is also an inevitability. And it seems inevitable that the devil should have chosen that day on which to appear, just for a little, in a busy city street. I think that he did not come to challenge me, nor to work his own havoc, but rather to share for a moment the soul of humanity, to see for himself the dark

1

spaces at the centre of my mind. There can be little doubt that it was us who attracted him there. In a way it was us who created him.

But this is a hard story to tell, of how I met the devil and how I lost him again—though there was little that I did not lose along the way—and we must begin on a June evening of a summer not so long ago. An evening when neither the past nor the future were within my boundaries of comprehension.

Chapter One

That June, up until about the middle of the month, we did nothing but joke and drink and stare into the endless sky. Throughout the daylight hours the university campus was hazy with the smell of sun lotion and the shifting dreams of a thousand restless minds, rising at nightfall to dance among the whispers of the stars. There were evenings when we would wander down, across the tired pathway, to where a bright student bar pulsated with music. Sitting outside on the cooling patio, where the clank of glasses struck a homely note, it seemed that the world was spinning through an endless illusion of our own creation.

And there were mornings when I awoke and had only to move my head to feel the poison of the previous night's drinking bout coursing through my body, with half-formed regrets streaming from every thought—but even then it did not last long and by early noon there was no more pain. These were the final days of my first year at university—a mist of alcohol, heat and noise. For two weeks after the exams were finished we remained in our halls of residence and it was an occasion to re-enact all that had taken place over the past nine months.

In between times we used to talk about our plans for the summer. Some people were going to work, some were going to travel, and still others had no idea of what they were going to do. Perhaps that was the best arrangement, to be completely unsure of what the oncoming months would bring. That way there was nothing to hope for and nothing much to fear. But I belonged to the second group, and the adventure to which I was now drawing very close had been haunting me for weeks.

It had long before become clear to me that there were hard times ahead. Frequently I was swept by a feeling of great sadness, something too dull to be called pain that stirred in my chest when I looked out of my window, beyond the university, to where the gentle green hills rolled away into the distance. Sometimes, when I thought of Eva, all I wanted to do was cry.

Ever since we had started dating Eva had been a problem to me, in the way that a girlfriend or boyfriend is a problem for everyone. Yet ours was a particularly difficult relationship. She was a German student who had been studying in England until the end of March when she had returned home to complete her degree. We had fallen together at a party, just a few weeks before she was due to leave, and had spent two heady, uncertain weeks of confused emotions wondering whether or not we had any future, and gradually finding ourselves more and more deeply in love. When she left we had agreed that I should visit her as soon as my year at university finished, and for the last two and a half months I had been signing my letters and e-mails to her 'love Dave,' or 'love you lots, Dave.' Her replies were usually warm enough to convince me that she cared as much for me as I did for her, but I still worried unceasingly and analysed every sentence for a possible cooling of feeling.

I had booked a coach ticket to travel to Germany near the start of June, but as the day approached for me to leave I began to miss her more and more, until the time that we had spent together seemed that it had been a kind of dream, and that by making the journey to visit her I should be stepping back into that dream. I do not know for sure why it all felt so unreal, so terribly poetic. Perhaps it was something to do with the fact that we began dating just as the spring had arrived, that we would walk down the lanes and pathways around the university with the daffodils opening and every hedgerow filled with expectant life. It was very much like a youthful vision becoming reality—as when a child walks home from school in springtime and wonders at the great sense of living, of coming into being, that is present in everything, realising one day that what we sense in the land and air can live in our feelings and hopes. And now I found myself full of apprehension and painful love, desperate for the future yet also deeply afraid of it.

The conversation that I held with two of my closest friends on the evening before the end of term proved the extent to which I was unable to discuss the worries that haunted me. Big, friendly Jason and half-crazy Dan were sitting in my room which was now full of boxes, all packed and ready to be taken home the next day.

'It feels so weird to think that the year's gone already,' said Jason as he shifted in the chair.

'I think it's been long enough,' Dan replied, 'too long in some ways. I'm looking forward to getting away.'

'What are you going to do over the holiday?'

'Work, I guess.'

'What work's that?' I asked, surprised at hearing such an ambitious statement from a man whose idea of a hard day's labour was to wake up around midday and perhaps wander to the library to read for half an hour in the late afternoon.

'Important scientific work. I'm hoping to make a major breakthrough before September.'

'I see.' I didn't bother to ask exactly what scientific work he was involved in. Dan was always making big plans for the future but they never came to anything.

'When are you going to Germany?' Jason asked.

'In one week's time. I'm leaving on Saturday and arriving back two weeks later.'

'I bet you can't wait to see your girlfriend again,' said Dan with a distant expression in his eyes.

'Of course not. It'll be exciting to travel as well.' I wished that I could explain to my friends how I really felt—how I was terrified that Eva might have changed or decided that our relationship was too complicated to be worthwhile, how I was afraid of the pain that would come when we had to part again.

'What's your German like, have you learnt any?' Dan asked.

'A bit, but I'm not very good.' That was another worry and another lie. Ever since Eva had returned home I had wanted to learn some German but had never quite managed to start.

'You've been to Germany, haven't you, Dan?' Jason asked.

'Yes, it was a couple of years ago. I went on a college trip.'

'What was it like?' I asked.

'It was pretty good. It would have been better if I hadn't been with the college though.'

'I'm not sure about that,' Jason laughed, 'I can't bear to think about you being unrestrained in a foreign place—they may never have let any more English people into the country, and where would Dave be then?'

'Do you think that people in Germany are going to mind an Englishman wandering around in their midst?' I asked jokingly but meaning it seriously.

'You mean, will you get attacked by deranged nationalists? I doubt it—I'm sure most Germans have seen a foreigner at some point.' Dan looked at me and saw deeper than I imagined he could. 'It's always a bit scary when you go to a new country for the first time, especially when the people there speak a different language, but you'll be fine because you've got your girlfriend to look after you.'

'I guess I'm more of a country boy,' I agreed. 'Going to a big city frightens me.'

'Are you going to see Jens at all whilst you're away?' Jason asked with a sudden glow in his eyes.

'Yes, definitely. I shall probably spend a night at his house at some point.' Jens was another German student who had been studying with us during the first term. He had been a good friend to us all, full of jokes and adventure, and the loss of such a valuable crony half way through the year had naturally been a sad one. However, Jens lived very close to Eva and I was looking forward to catching up with him at some point.

'There you go then,' Dan cried triumphantly, 'you know two people out there and you'll probably quickly meet a lot more.'

'This is where I'm going,' I said, unfolding a map of Europe that had been packed on top of a box and pointing out the city where Eva lived.

'Not far from Munich,' said Jason. 'You should go and visit an even bigger city.'

'We might go to Munich,' I agreed, 'but we don't really have a lot of time. Eva's still at university at the moment so she'll have to be working quite a lot while I'm there.'

'You're going to put her off then,' Jason smiled, 'that's good. I think that the best thing about being in a relationship is that your partner can put you off working, just at the right moments. Many a time I've been about to put pen to paper and thought to myself that if only I had somebody who really cared for me then they would phone me up and save me.'

'The secret is to give up any hope of ever doing anything useful,' Dan spoke with confidence, 'if you can start each day with no expectations then you can't ever be disappointed, and any work you do manage is some fine achievement.'

'Well then, shall we go for a drink?' I asked, having glanced outside and noticed the fading light, with the sorrowful evening chorus beginning in the trees.

'Of course,' Dan replied, 'I will have a number of drinks—by rights we should have been on our way to some grotty nightclub at this very moment.'

'I just don't feel like going out anywhere much tonight, what with leaving early in the morning,' Jason apologised. I felt nothing but thankfulness that he had taken this attitude. Almost every Friday we would go out to a nightclub, and almost every Friday I would hate it. The noise, the confusion, the masses of people stuffed onto a tiny dance-floor, the aggressive drunk men and the hysterical girls, the thousands of people having to drink enough alcohol to convince themselves that they were having a good time. And we paid for all this—paid money to put ourselves in a warlike situation once a week that we all pretended to enjoy. I would much rather go out to a nearby bar and have a few drinks there, without having to experience the closest thing to hell that we had managed to create in our day-to-day lives.

'It's a shame we can't go to a club,' I said, with that inner glow of somebody who has had his own way through another person's suggestion, 'but we might as well go out somewhere.'

In the end we just went to the nearest student bar on campus and had a few drinks, but it was strange because we were all going away the next day and it was a bit sad and difficult to make conversation.

'Odd how you miss the past, even if you didn't always enjoy it,' said Dan, feeling the general mood of the gathering.

'Absolutely,' I agreed. He was right, of course. Almost from my very first day at university I had looked forward to having a long break from student life, but now it was suddenly something that I would miss, even though we would all return in a few months. But half my mind was on other matters. The table we were sitting at was the one where I had once sat with Eva on a distant, hazy evening and become suddenly aware of how much a central part of my life she had become. It had been a warm day and the twilight was glowing on the patio beyond the window. We were holding hands and talking so that it was nice just to be together, and I had realised then all the painful love that the future held—all the worries of her going away and the struggles that we would face, contained within that one moment when I looked into her eyes and saw that we had become a couple, and that our lives were irrevocably tied through a desire to self-sacrifice and a closeness of understanding.

'It seems so long ago,' I said to myself, 'I wish that Eva were here now.' And, throughout my life, I have hardly wished more sincerely for anything but that she should have been there on that last night of the term. From the bar window I could see the open fields rushing away through the distance until they faded into the red evening. It seemed hugely unkind that she should be so far away, in another country, beyond the limits of my knowledge — but at the same time I was swept by such a huge, desperate desire to see her again that seemed to override all other considerations and worries.

'I'm suddenly starting to look forward to my trip,' I said out loud.

'Of course you are,' Dan smiled, 'there's nothing to be afraid of.'

Those few moments in the bar were ones in which the more adventurous side of my character appeared, and I began to see the trials ahead as a kind of game that could be won or lost but that it was good to have played either way. Nevertheless, I still experienced a sharp jab of nerves and sadness as I said goodbye to my friends until September and watched them walk away into the night, leaving me to face my summer alone.

It was a strange week that I spent at home — one of those dreadful periods of waiting when it is impossible to turn the mind to anything other than the coming event. The day before leaving I spoke to Eva on the phone to ensure that everything was still all right, and we had a short but pleasant conversation.

'Anyway,' she said after we had been speaking for ten minutes, 'I'd better go now, but we can see each other in two days.' And those words brought such a rush of happiness into my soul that I began actively looking forward to the journey once again. It was hard to believe that in just two days we would be back together, and hopefully could continue from where we had ended in March. With such thoughts in mind I began to pack. Having always travelled light I wanted to make sure that all my luggage would fit into one, small suitcase. After a time spent rearranging items the lid was closed, and I next placed a few essentials into a separate bag for hand luggage. There was a stab of nervous excitement as I added my passport — a kind of symbol for this first trip abroad that I was to make alone. Finally I double-checked the time of travel on my coach ticket. Ten o'clock the following evening. It was to be a sixteen-hour coach trip, arriving in Frankfurt the following afternoon where I would meet Eva, and from where we would take a train back to her home city. An exhausting journey. And as I sat on the floor with my suitcase all packed and ready to go, I was torn between a desire to hurry to Germany and let the future unfold, and a strange longing to be back in the days of my childhood, before such emotional pursuits had become necessary and when summer meant simply a long break from classes.

The next day a friend gave me a lift to the London coach station. As we drove through the city it seemed to be such a huge, bleak place, full of endless tiny shops and dirty, aggressive roads. I wondered how anybody could flourish within such a soulless environment, but then of course it is impossible to understand a community from the outside. On saying goodbye to my friend at the entrance to the coach station I felt very much like I had when being dropped off for my first day at secondary school—that sense of being a little lost and unsure as to what is about to happen. There were throngs of people crowding everywhere, sometimes coming very close to actually shoving one another out of the way, yet there were still pigeons hopping around, looking so battered and weary within the dank smell of their surroundings. More than anything else at that moment I wished that I had a travelling companion, somebody with whom I could talk and joke, share the discomforts and confer with when it came to making decisions.

On my ticket were printed a number of instructions, one of which mentioned that it was necessary to check in before making an overseas trip. I had arrived an hour and a half before departure time to make sure that I didn't have to hurry.

'Do you know where the check-in place is for European destinations?' I asked a jovial-looking guard.

'Right through there,' he replied, pointing to a door a short distance away. Pushing between the masses I found the check-in queue. It was a long line of nervous people, all with bags and suitcases of varying size. Every few moments the queue moved forward and there were a collection of slithers and bangs as baggage was shifted along by its owners. After a long wait I was asked to show my passport before being directed to the correct bay where a group of fellow passengers were already standing.

There was still half an hour before the coach was set to leave, and it passed very slowly. I began to feel tired, the kind of tiredness that is so often felt before setting out on a long journey, with the back of my mind contemplating the many unknowns ahead. Every minute or so I glanced at my watch while more people gathered, and all throughout there was the rumble and hiss of the big coaches arriving and departing.

Eventually the driver appeared and the group around me gathered up their bags.

'How far are you going?' a middle-aged man asked a young woman.

'Just as far as Brussels. How about you?'

'I'm heading to Munich to visit family.'

As our tickets were checked and our luggage loaded I wondered where all the different people boarding the coach were going, and why they were going there. So many stories could be told about that one, small gathering, but it was my own story that I could sense unfolding as we reversed out of the bay to begin our journey, and my own, personal trip into the long awaited future.

Chapter Two

We left the coach station and began a long passage through the London streets, past endless kebab shops and small stores, bound for Dover and the ferry port. It was a restless night, the anger and passion of the long, hot day faded into an impatient darkness, and it took us a long time to squeeze our way out of the city, every occasional burst of speed ending with a traffic light or a tight corner. I tried to avoid thinking too much about potential problems—namely my fear of boarding the wrong coach after the ferry crossing to Calais, and the dread that somehow Eva would fail to meet me at Frankfurt and I would be stranded in a foreign city with no means of communication. Opening my wallet, I checked that the piece of paper bearing the phone numbers of both Eva and Jens was still tucked safely away in case of emergency. Dan was right, it certainly was a comfort to have more than one contact when travelling abroad.

During my preparations I had often wondered who would sit next to me during the trip, but so far the seat to my right was unoccupied and the coach was little over half full. A family sat before me, the mother and child on the seat in front with the father and another child sitting opposite them. Although I could tell that they were speaking French, I had no idea as to what they were saying. It probably wasn't anything very exciting though, there seemed to be so little that could be said at the start of such a long haul. Further up the vehicle a child was crying.

From time to time as I gazed out the window I caught a glimpse of the city sky, fading into blackness as it rushed towards the stars. It was an unsettling sight—there was some kind of blackness that I was heading towards, the uncharted dreams that would finally be opened. There was fear out there, hidden somewhere in the night, beyond the warm glow of a million dwellings and the security of home.

We left London behind us, discreet in its sudden end as we merged with the speeding mass of the motorway, like a rocket breaking free of the Earth's gravity. Away from the city restraints the constant drone of traffic created a hypnotic air. I tried to imagine what the scenery would be like in Europe, whether it would be similar to the English countryside, but somehow I was not in an imaginative mood, and there was little to think of besides my immediate surroundings. It was oddly brain numbing to sit perfectly still while outside the dark world rushed past, as if the interior of the vehicle had been suspended from time and reality.

'What kind of crisps have you brought?' I heard a male voice behind me ask.

'Just plain,' a female voice relied, 'is that okay?'

'I suppose so.' A few moments later the sound of munching began. My hand luggage contained a few sandwiches and some crisps as well as water, but I wasn't feeling hungry.

The child stopped crying and I guessed that it was probably asleep. From time to time I felt drowsy myself; it was hot on the coach and quite airless. When I closed my eyes it seemed that my head was resting on a pillow and that there were sheets drawn over me, that I was back home in my own bed, drifting away into a dream with the flowing rhythm of the passing traffic—then my head jerked up as I broke away from the half-dream and was back on the coach, my hand brushing against the cold glass of the window, and the seat in front too near and claustrophobic. My forehead felt irritatingly greasy and I longed for a good shower and a bed.

Eventually we arrived at Dover, and the baby began to cry again as we approached the terminal. Soon the coach had been loaded onto the ferry and we were told to leave the vehicle, most people evidently looking forward to a chance to stretch their legs on the boat. One young man of about my age spoke to me in German as we dismounted.

'Sorry?' Once again there was a stab of guilt, as I wished that I had spent at least a little time learning some German.

'I said that it's been a very good journey so far,' he repeated in English.

'Yes, yes, not too many hold-ups in London.'

'You're not German then?' he asked, rather unnecessarily I thought.

'No, I'm going to Germany though, to visit a friend. How about you?'

'My parents live in Hamburg but I'm at college in England.' He drifted away and began speaking with another man. I made a short exploration of the ship, walking down the carpeted corridors and occasionally peering out into the dark sea, a blackness of nerves and excitement. Silently we were slicing though the water and drawing ever closer to the continent, though I could hardly believe it. Standing in the brightly lit corridor, I could think only of the journey and the miles still to be crossed. Eva felt as distant as ever.

It was pleasant to be able to stroll around, but after a while I found a fast-food lounge and bought a coffee, sitting at a table from which I could keep an eye on several other passengers from my coach. I had made up my mind to try and keep at least one of my fellow travellers in sight so that there would be no chance of accidentally boarding the wrong vehicle. In fact this was more of a nightmare development than a real possibility as the coach was parked at the end of its row and was very obvious, but my overimaginative mind had been busily constructing worst-case scenarios all week until they began to seem quite feasible.

I glanced around at the occupants of other tables and noticed that the lounge did not have the relaxed atmosphere of a coffee shop or tearoom. Everybody was slightly on edge, unable to forget that they were in the middle of the journey and always with half a mind on the imminent order to return to the coaches. It had more the feel of a railway station refreshments room. Indeed, after taking a few sips of coffee I saw what appeared to be a madman, sitting alone in a corner and holding a conversation with himself whilst making excessive arm gestures.

'I'll bet they do,' he said, 'and what's more, I've heard that Brian agrees. He was up in London recently.' There was a pause during which he appeared to be listening intently to someone I couldn't see, and then, 'Yes, of course. New York is always possible, but check it out with the big man first.'

About a minute passed before I realised that he was talking into a hands-free mobile phone. Although it was a relief to find that he was not speaking to himself, I wondered whether the desire to sit in a room full of people and bawl out one half of a business conversation would really count as sanity. I drank the rest of my coffee whilst speculating on how long the crossing would take. Now that several hours had passed since leaving London, I found that I was not tired at all, though I guessed that this was due to being able to move freely about again.

'Better watch out for the big guns,' the man in corner advised his invisible colleague. I began to think of Eva again.

The worst point about her departure the previous March was that it had left me very confused as to what the future held. If only we had been able talk more about our problems then everything could be so much easier, but we had never really discussed what we thought, or even what we hoped would happen after that bright, surreal moment when we said goodbye. It had been so warm and pleasant that day, but the daffodils at the roadside did not seem fitting for such an occasion—how strange that she should vanish into a spring morning and leave only the ashes of memory behind with so many important words unsaid.

Since then nothing, no telephone call or letter, had been satisfying. Frozen words on a page were not enough to bring a sense of closeness, and our hasty phone calls left me all the more lonely after the receiver was replaced and the line between us broken. And, as time passed, I found that there were other insecurities besides our unclear relationship. Eva was a very attractive girl, and this began to work at my mind until I imagined her constantly being approached by other men, eager for romance. Every time she wrote that she had been to a nightclub or had been talking with a male friend it caused a sickening jealousy to rise in my chest. Many times I had stood paralysed by my reflection in a mirror, noticing how thin I was and wondering how Eva could ever be attracted to me when there were so many other men around her every day.

'Great, so give him a buzz and find out,' my friend in the corner shouted. I looked up at him just as he glanced at me, and our eyes met for an uncomfortable, lingering moment. Peering into my empty cup, I pretended to find it deeply interesting. A few moments later, when the announcement was made that we would shortly be arriving at Calais, I was glad for the excuse to leave my seat. Finding the correct coach was no difficulty, though I made sure that the same French-speaking family were sitting in front of me. The crisp eating pair behind also returned to their places, the man middle aged and balding with his companion a good ten years younger and looking far livelier.

'Exciting to be on the Continent again,' I heard her remark as they squeezed into their seats.

'I'd rather be at home in bed.'

'Oh hush.' Their conversation ended and I suddenly felt very hungry. I ate one cheese sandwich and a packet of crisps, the cheese tasting as though it were half melted and the two slices of bread crushed tightly together and damp. The coach felt cramped and uncomfortable, and I hoped the hours would pass quickly.

Calais did not detain us for long and soon we were pressing forward into the night. All was silent save for an occasional bleep or thud, and it seemed that I was one of the few passengers who was not asleep. Down the central aisle the air was heavy with slumber on either side—hunched bodies occasionally twitching a limb, minds drifting through their own imaginary lands. A few hours dragged along and the darkness began to yield until, as we passed through Brussels, the first glimmers of dawn began to open the city. Tall stately buildings of a thousand windows peered down into the gloom with a benevolent gaze, and the deserted streets held a feeling of ease and quiet confidence. The modern air of the zone was comfortably at peace in its coming together with the freshness of early morning, a gentle opening to a day that would soon be full of bustle and rush.

We stopped at the coach station and the French-speaking family departed, along with a number of other passengers. More people boarded and two middle-aged women occupied the seats in front of me. Outside, a man on a bike passed through my line of vision and I idly wondered what his business was in being about so early.

'How long is this part of the journey going to take?' one of the women in front asked.

'Some hours. I think we should have gone by train,' her companion replied. They both spoke with American accents.

'Well, at least we get more scenery this way.'

'No, we get the same scenery but longer to look at it.'

'I prefer coach travel anyway.' They were still arguing the point as we left Brussels, past one or two parks and more large building before rejoining the wide road.

So we rolled on, through flat, green fields, now at the stage of the journey where time becomes a numbness that sinks below reality. The landscape was not dramatic, but on occasion a part of it—now a broken tree, now a cracked mud track—would trigger a memory of bygone moments. So much of the countryside was similar to that which I knew from home that it would, at times, put me in mind of summer days spent far away and years before; summers when the troubles of the world had ceased with the break-up from school, and the desires of the moment went nowhere beyond a cricket bat or a dreaming wood. We passed a field spotted with poppies, holding my attention for a few moments before we left it behind forever. There was something tragic in the scene—green-brown grass and the hazy red mist; I began to think of the Great War and to wonder whether these fields had ever known slaughter, deaths that had faded now almost to the unknown.

Poppies whose roots are in man's veins
Drop, and are ever dropping;
But mine in my ear is safe,
Just a little white with the dust.

It occurred to me that we were passing through history just as briefly as those who had died in the war. One day there would be nobody left to remember this little group of passengers who had swept through these fields on a summer morning, and it would be as though the moment with all its worries and hopes had never existed.

Hours came and went without incident, until around mid-morning we stopped at a roadside shop and café. Again, I was glad of the chance to escape from the coach for a little, though the rest was only to be for quarter of an hour. Having found the toilets in the café I glanced around the shop and, noticing the price labels, it occurred to me that we had entered Germany. After a while I went outside to where most of the passengers had gathered to smoke around the front of the coach, and after a few moments a man of late middle age caught my eye and asked me where I was going.

'Does the coach go directly there?' he asked when I told him.

'No, I'm going to have to catch a train from Frankfurt. A friend's meeting me at the station.' I felt a rush of excitement at the thought of meeting Eva.

'That's good. Actually I've been several times where you're headed. It's a lovely place. Bavaria's my favourite part of Germany, and your city's very interesting.'

'It's a nice city then?'

'Well, like any town it has good parts and not so good parts. Lots of history, castles and that sort of thing.' He fell silent for a moment.

'How much longer till we reach Frankfurt do you suppose?' I asked, leaning against the low wall and feeling the roughness of the concrete beneath my fingers.

'A few hours I suppose, perhaps three or four. Have you set your watch to German time yet?'

'Yes, I did it on the ferry. One hour forward, isn't it?'

'That's right.' He was silent again as overhead two black birds squawked across the sky, disappearing behind the roof of the building.

'Hot, isn't it?' I said eventually, noticing the high temperature for the first time myself.

'I thought it would be. We have a few months of sunshine ahead of us. Excuse me.' He pardoned himself and went into the café.

I stood on my own, and looking around it was interesting to see how temporary bonds were being formed between certain passengers. Some now stood in the same groups that they had formed on the ferry, some were in pairs and others alone. I was beginning to recognise the different faces and even to put a little character into them. As well as those few with whom I had held a conversation and the occupants of the seats in front and behind me, there were a number of people who had become an essential part of the group—a plump, jolly man in his late thirties, a small grandmotherly woman of about sixty years, an eager student—all were members of an odd community that bound us together for the duration of the trip. It was hard to imagine them departing.

'Time to continue,' the driver announced in uncertain English. He had taken over from the original driver at Brussels and I wondered how often he made the same route, ferrying a few dozen passengers across the continent and back into their various lives.

The minutes passed very quickly as we began the final part of the journey to Frankfurt, but when I realised that there was only an hour or so until arrival, everything slowed down. The landscape was subtly different from that of home, but not massively so, and it seemed more unreal than ever that I was about to see Eva again. All worries about meeting at the correct time and place vanished as I began to wonder what it would be like to be together once more.

Trees and wide fields passed by the window, baked by a sun which seemed to shine with twice the intensity that it had done in England, until at last the maze of countryside was navigated as we left the motorway and entered Frankfurt, the outskirts of small buildings and traffic lights drawing us further towards its heart. Soon we passed a large carnival aglow with brightly coloured tents and children clutching balloons; I wondered whether we had almost reached the coach station and examined, as best I could, every pedestrian in case I should catch a glimpse of Eva walking to meet me, but soon we had passed the stalls and their lively attractions and were heading deeper into the city.

In the end it must have taken us half an hour to reach the coach station from the edge of Frankfurt. As it became obvious that we were about to arrive my heart began to beat very quickly with the nerves of waiting. We slowed down on a road with several other coaches parked along it and I could see no sign of Eva, but then, swinging right around to face the opposite direction, we drove back down the other side of the road before pulling into a parking space. The driver reminded everybody leaving the coach to take their belongings with them, and just as the doors hissed open I caught sight of Eva. She was standing a few metres away and waved, having noticed me at the same moment. In the few instants that my eyes rested on her all the anxiety of the past months dissolved in a great rush of tenderness—suddenly I was experiencing emotions that had remained frozen since March and which I had been unable to recall precisely when we were apart. She was lovelier than ever in a long summer skirt and light blouse, and it seemed that every curve of her body, every wisp of her hair, was a giddy perfection. Leaving my seat I walked unhurriedly down the central aisle, pausing for a moment before descending the stairs, taking pleasure in the drama of the moment. She was waiting just outside the door and we hugged each other before speaking. Feeling her body pressed against mine brought more than the warmth of physical closeness for at that moment our souls were close as well, as if the cold months of separation were melting away until there was nothing left but our own world and our own dreams, stretching blissfully to the horizons.

'How was the journey?' she asked after a pause in which we both wondered what to say.

'Fine, though rather long. Did you have to leave early to get here?'

'Yes, I arrived a few hours ago. I haven't explored the city much.'

'This is your first time in Frankfurt as well, isn't it?'

'I've only been through before.'

'A new experience for both of us then.' I glowed with the confidence of the conquering spirit, glancing back at the coach and catching the eye of the plump, jovial man who gave me a knowing grin. What fabulous people, I thought. What a brilliant, colourful world exists for those who dare to seek it. Every sight and sense, from the shimmering tarmac road to the sweeping rush of the sky, welcomed me into a new chance and a new happiness.

'Shall we get lunch? I haven't eaten since breakfast.' Eva pointed towards the nearby building. 'That's the train station as well as the coach centre and they have some fast-food places inside.'

'Good idea, I've only eaten a sandwich since London. I'll just get my luggage.' It was with a jubilant gaze that I greeted the afternoon city and all its glowing life.

Chapter Three

After collecting my luggage and thanking the driver we entered the cool, crowded station and found a fast-food restaurant. It was busy at the counter where the orders were placed and my suitcase was awkward to hold without buffeting people.

'What do you want to eat?' Eva asked. I left my order with her and went to find a table. At first there didn't appear to even be any unoccupied seats, but then a family in the corner stood up to leave and I took their place, Eva joining me with the food a few minutes later. As she walked towards me I noticed that her skirt had a large slit almost up its entire length. It made her look fiendishly desirable, and I felt proud that she was with me, hoping that people would notice us together. Yet I was a little surprised that she would wear such a revealing outfit.

'What time are we going to catch the train home?' I asked after we had been eating for a while.

'I don't mind. There are trains every few hours or so.'

'We can check the times later then. Do you have any plans for what we should do tomorrow?'

'Well, at some point we must visit the beer festival.'

'What's that?'

'I thought I had already mentioned it. One of the nearby towns is holding its annual beer festival at the moment; it lasts two weeks.' She scooped the last few chips into her mouth.

'Perhaps you did mention it, I may have forgotten.'

'Yesterday was the opening night; I went in the evening. It's in the same town as my university.'

'What was it like?'

'Crazy as normal. Everybody was dancing on the tables, then some of the men picked up one of the benches while there were people dancing on it and started swinging it from side to side.'

'Sounds great,' I lied. It appeared that more personal demons would have to be confronted than I had anticipated — the festival sounded worryingly like a wild nightclub—but it was important to appear enthusiastic. 'Well, we must certainly go there at some point.'

Chairs squeaked against the floor as people around us arrived and departed. Watching Eva taking sips from her drink I considered how strange it was that, in the same moment, I could neither quite believe that she was with me nor imagine that we had ever been apart. I smiled to myself, thinking how shallow our conversation would sound to an outsider. Because English was not Eva's first language, we seldom managed to have really flowing conversations, yet somehow that didn't seem to matter too much.

'There's something you have to know,' she said, suddenly serious, eyes staring straight into mine.

'Yes?'

'My mother's very ill at the moment.'

'I'm sorry to hear that.'

'It's just old age really, and she's never been well since my father died. She can hardly get out of the house now.'

'So you need to visit her a lot. That's no problem, she only lives about ten minutes' walk from your flat, doesn't she?'

'Yes, but it's not only that,' her eyes still intensely focused into mine, 'I don't think that you should meet her. She doesn't know about you yet, and I want to keep your visit a secret.'

'Why?'

'Because I don't want to cause her a shock.'

'Shock?'

'It's just that you're so much younger than me, it might shock her.'

'I see.' She was right in a sense. The fact that Eva was nearly ten years my senior was something which I hid from myself wherever possible, and was certainly not at issue that could be discussed with anybody else. Because her age was not apparent, none of my friends had been aware of the gap, but it still left a feeling of undeserved guilt, as if we were doing something wrong and having to lie about it.

'Eva, I think it would be best if you didn't have to lie to your mother.'

'I won't have to lie, I just won't mention you.'

'That's the whole point—it doesn't make me feel very special, having to live like a fugitive. I want to be accepted by your family.'

'Oh, it's not that my mother wouldn't like you. She's a really lovely person, just I don't want to risk shocking her.'

'Well, let's see how things go.' I wanted to discuss the problem further but I couldn't think of the right words and didn't want to cause an argument. I had been counting on meeting Eva's family, knowing that if they were aware of our relationship it would make me feel a great deal more secure.

'So none of your relations know about me?' I asked, sucking the remnants of my drink through the spluttering straw.

'Only my mother lives nearby. I don't have much contact with the rest of the family.' That was enough to make the point—our relationship was a secret and destined to remain as one.

There was an uncomfortable silence as we both regretted the past conversation. After a while we left the restaurant and went to the station to check the train times.

'One leaves in twenty minutes,' Eva said as she traced her finger across the timetable, 'or there's one leaving in two and a half hours.'

'I'm actually quite tired. What is there to see in Frankfurt?' I was desperate to reach Eva's flat where I could rest, but didn't want to appear boring.

'I'm not sure. We could have a look around the city if you want.'

'Perhaps it would be easier if we caught the earlier train. I'm pretty exhausted.'

'Okay, if you want.'

It was very busy on the platform so we stood waiting and watched the crowds move around us. Many languages floated around us from people of different races and nations, yet despite this multicultural atmosphere I still felt like an alien, somehow embarrassed to be foreign. There were suitcases and sometimes trolleys piled high with luggage, men and women squeezing their way past one another in bad humour and confusion. As my gaze wondered to a pair of squabbling children Eva suddenly grabbed my arm, pulling me a few steps to one side.

'What's the matter?'

'That man spoke to me again.' She peered through the crowds and relaxed a little.

'What man?'

'I think he's gone. Yes, he's going away from the platform. I don't think he's catching this train.'

'Why, what did he say?' I looked around but could not see who she was talking about.

'He kept talking to me earlier on, asking if I was free tonight.'

'Really? Well, he's gone now.' Jealousy poured through my body as I wondered whether this was a common experience for Eva when I was away. Although she had ignored him, the very thought that another man had approached her was enough to make my stomach quiver. I tried to forget the incident, but it was difficult.

After another minute the train arrived and we climbed aboard. We sat alone in our carriage of sixteen seats, which was surprising because it had been so busy on the platform. Eva sat facing me, absentmindedly running her fingers through her hair. The city vanished and once again there was countryside flying past the window. I was very tired.

'I'll have to phone Jens soon,' I said eventually.

'Yes, of course. Perhaps he can come to the festival with us one time.'

'That would be good.'

It was a long journey as we had bought cheap tickets and had to take a slow train. After a couple of hours the landscape changed and we began to pass mountains. Perhaps it was simply because I was so weary, but as I looked up at the rocky peaks they seemed somehow to be a part of a fairytale, a different reality — vast fortresses of enchantment from a half recalled daydream. And as we pushed further south I examined a small map of the region, and the Germanic names of the towns, Hosbach, Würzberg, Kitzingen, were something from the distant past, from a mystical age that I had been unwittingly entrapped within. I could almost feel the gaze of ancient peoples, watching us coldly as we sped on east toward our future.

'I've had an idea,' Eva spoke with a mischievous shine in her eyes.

'What's that?'

'On the way home we could stop at the festival.'

'We could.' This was exactly the suggestion that I had feared, but I felt unable to disappoint her. 'Are you sure that you can manage two nights in a row?'

'I don't mind. It's on the way home anyway.'

'Okay then, let's go there, but we won't stay very long.'

'I've never been two nights in a row before,' she smiled and rearranged the skirt over her knees before allowing her gaze to drift back to the scenery. Once again, I experienced a huge sense of physical attraction towards her, a great desire to hold her in my arms, but the time was not yet right; I could tell that it would take a while for her to grow comfortable with me again. Then the man at the station crossed my mind and the jealousy rose within me again — in just two weeks I would have to return to England and there was little time to waste.

'We're nearly there,' Eva told me after another two hours had passed and the mountains disappeared to be replaced by trees, 'this little forest is about ten minutes from our stop.'

'What are we going to do about my suitcase?' I asked. 'I can't take it with me, it'll get in the way.'

'Yes, I know. You can leave it in one of the lockers at the station.'

We continued to roll along the last, nervous stretch of track, trees blurred in a dazzle of green and brown. I wished that Eva had suggested a straight trip back to her flat—it occurred to me that it was over twenty-four hours since I had left home.

When we arrived at the station, stepping out into the warm evening, a warning sign as to what lay ahead was awaiting us. From the distance came drunken shouts, drawing closer until a group of men reeled into sight, staggering their way towards a platform. They plunged into a train and, as we passed close by, one of them thrust his head out of the window and shouted something to us which caused a great roar to go up from within the carriage.

'They say that I should go with them,' Eva smiled, 'they've just been at the festival.' My heart fluttered a little as I wondered whether similar events had occurred on the previous night. Suddenly I realised what an easy target she must seem for some men, showing off her legs with that skirt. I felt hot and angry to think that they had even looked at her, as though she were a piece of artwork to be admired.

We walked on, down a flight of concrete steps and into a room full of lockers. The place felt threatening and I was relieved that there were no drunks within the confined space. It cost five marks to secure my suitcase and coat, the money inserted and the key released by twisting a dial.

'What are the chances that it'll still be there when we get back?' I pondered, examining the lock.

'It's more likely that you'll loose the key. Let's go back up.'

We walked back through the station and out to the park where the festival was being held. It was a huge event, the streets heaving with men and women of all ages on their way to or from the show. In the park itself the crowds were even denser as we squeezed along the main path; a wide gravel track along the whole length of which were a variety of enormous open fronted tents, filled with the clamour of loud music and crashing beer mugs. I was terrified.

'We'll go to the same place that I went to last night,' Eva shouted, after about five minutes turning to the left into a tent slightly larger than the others. Inside, we found pandemonium. There was no covering on the floor and the grass had been trodden down into a muddy pulp. A band played on a stage at the far end some hundred metres away, its members dressed in Bavarian costume, beneath which men carried trays of beer between the rows of benches covering almost the entire ground space. These benches had enough room for six or seven people to sit along either side, and almost every one of the countless dozens was occupied by a roaring, swilling crowd, some sitting, some dancing. The air pulsated with noise and alcohol, fear and heat, like a mouth of hell to my weary mind.

Eva said that she needed a drink before being able to dance and we bought a large, litre mug to share.

'How much did it cost?' I asked, taking a couple of notes from my wallet.

'Just over ten marks.'

'I'd better pay for it, as you bought lunch.' I handed her two five mark notes and we began to drink the beer, standing to one side of the stage where it was fairly quiet. It was a little recess, peaceful and almost cosy, and I hoped that we could remain there and enjoy the music without having to enter the packed main area, but as soon as the drink was finished Eva announced that we were going to dance, and began to push her way back between the benches. There did not appear to be any free seats so we stood at the end of one aisle, waiting to see if anybody left.

'We might as well dance here for a bit,' Eva decided, and abruptly began swinging her arms and body in a manner which suggested that she had drunk a lot more than half a litre. I attempted to follow her example, but it was incredibly embarrassing — there was nobody else dancing near us, and people gave irritated glares as they walked past. I felt horribly sober.

'Shall we go and find somewhere to sit?' I asked after five minutes, the embarrassment built to the level where I was practically rooted to the spot.

'Okay then.' Eva began to run from bench to bench, brimming over with energy, until she found some free space. She was throwing herself fully into the party spirit while I longed to go home but was desperate not to let her know. The bench that we eventually sat at was mostly taken up by middle-aged men, three of whom sat opposite us. As we squeezed into the little space I felt sure that they were going to react angrily to our unwanted arrival, but in fact they seemed friendly enough, and began talking with Eva.

'They're from Austria,' she told me.

'You don't speak German then?' the first man asked me.

'No, not really.' It was strangely comforting to meet other foreigners. 'This is my first visit to Germany.'

'We work here,' the man replied.

'We say in this town that there are five seasons,' the second man said, looking up suddenly. 'Not the normal four seasons, but five. Spring, summer, autumn, winter and celebration time.'

'The celebration only lasts two weeks,' the third man joined. 'Not long enough.'

'It's plenty long enough for me,' said the first man.

I began to pick at the wood beneath my fingers, feeling a splinter lift before snapping free. The surface of the bench was rough where it had obviously been in use for a great many years. The band on the stage finished their final piece and were replaced by a different group amid loud cheering. The Austrian men stood up to leave.

'Remember,' the second man said, leaning towards me. 'Five seasons.'

As soon as they left, the most terrible phase of the evening began. I sat nearest to the aisle with Eva perched between me and another group of middle-aged men. They were all huge and boisterously drunk, and suddenly, with a great roar of enthusiasm, they rose to their feet and began to dance.

'Come on,' Eva grabbed my hand and pulled me up. The next hour was absolute torture. We danced, balanced precariously on the edge of the bench, yells and screams chocking the air, bodies twisting and leaping all around, violence hovering close by and ready to strike. A fight broke out a little distance away and security men rushed to the scene, pushing past the tight packed masses and causing an overflow wave of revellers to wash against our bench. As they receded again the man standing next to Eva tried to put his arm around her. She pulled back from him and, full of hot fear, I put my own arm around her shoulders in a protective gesture. The man winked at me and continued dancing, leaving me embarrassed, wondering how abnormal these feelings of jealousy were. And as we danced, with hell seemingly closing around us, I began to think that all my unnatural worries — cumulating in the fantasy that, at any time, somebody was going to seize Eva and carry her away into the darkness — could be banished if we were only able to talk to one another more freely, to express our concerns and desires outright. Most of all I wished that I could kiss her, that we could act more like a couple. I felt stupidly out of place.

A man with a huge red face climbed onto the bench and began to jump up and down, waving an empty beer mug. The bench tilted dangerously to one side and for a terrible moment it seemed that it must collapse, but somehow we survived and a security guard rushed over. The man was removed. Bands came and went on the stage, sometimes playing Bavarian folk music, sometimes modern pop. The alcohol-fuelled evening raged around us, now swelteringly hot and dry.

'We'd better go,' Eva unexpectedly spoke the welcome words, 'it shuts in a few minutes and we don't want to get caught in the rush.' Picking our way back through the tent we found that night had fallen and the area was bathed in bright, artificial lighting. The park and the streets were just as busy as they had been on our arrival, but now there was a more menacing atmosphere as groups of men shouted and kicked shattered mugs along the road.

'What do you want to do now?' Eva asked. I could see that there were long lines forming outside buildings that were obviously nightclubs, but enough was enough.

'I'd quite like to go home now. I'm really tired.'

'You don't want to go to a club then?'

'Well, we can always go another night. It wouldn't be good to use up all our energy on my first day here,' I said, glancing nervously around.

'I don't mind,' she spoke a little sternly, 'it's just that if you do want to go anywhere else you'll have to decide now.'

'Let's go home then.'

'Okay. You need to get your things from the locker.'

We retrieved my items and then went out to wait for a bus. There were crowds waiting with us and I felt horribly conspicuous and foreign, burdened by my suitcase. The concrete of the buildings nearby was ugly and menacing, and even the moon turned a frozen face towards us. The bus did not take long to arrive, but by the time we climbed aboard it was already packed with bodies and we were pressed against the luggage compartment with barely a handhold to avoid falling. The journey took about half an hour but it seemed to be never ending. Once again there was a riot of shouts and drunken laughter, but now it was all contained within a tiny space from which there was no escape. Every time somebody wanted to leave the bus it was necessary for them to wrestle their way to the doors, causing a chain reaction of disturbance to spread through the entire length of the vehicle. I felt sickeningly sure that a fight would start and we would be caught in the middle of it; I was so worried that I barely said a word to Eva the entire journey—somehow even looking at her made me feel more terrified that there would be trouble. The journey passed though and we crawled our way into the city of darkened streets. When we finally reached our destination about half of the remaining passengers disembarked as well, so it was not so difficult for us to leave.

'Now we just have to walk home,' Eva said as we hurried through the bus station. 'It takes about half an hour from here.

There is a bus that goes closer but I'm not sure whether it'll still be running at this time.'

'Better just to walk then.'

The streets were empty and, although we walked swiftly, it seemed to take us a long time to reach our destination. The silent roads could, in appearance, have almost belonged to any English city, yet I was intensely aware of being far from home, in an emotional sense as well as a physical one. This was the distant city that I had dreamed of as a child, the place that I had always woken from without knowing why I was there. There was something fearful still in the darkness—our footsteps seemed very loud through the warm, still air, and I felt uncomfortable with walking around so late at night, not knowing where we were. From time to time we passed a late night bar with lights still glowing and a few customers moving inside, and once a car full of teenagers screeched past us. When we finally arrived at Eva's flat I was very relieved.

The block of flats was a modern building, not outstanding in any way, yet not particularly ugly, having something of the feel of a university block of residence. Eva began to look nervous as we entered the dark corridor and took the lift up, and I couldn't help but feel that I was being smuggled in.

'This is my home,' she said, inviting me to investigate after carefully closing the door. It was a small flat with one bedroom, a sitting room, a kitchen and a bathroom. The kitchen window looked out over the street and the sitting room window, on the opposite side, looked over the garden and a little of the city.

'It's a lovely place,' I said. 'Do you have use of the garden?'

'It's a communal garden, but I don't go there much.'

'Yes, it's not very big for so many people.' I noticed that the flat had a distinctive smell, but couldn't place it, finally deciding that it was one of those individual odours which haunt most houses.

'Would you like any supper?' Eva asked from the kitchen.

'What do you have?'

'Cereal?'

'That'd be nice.'

We sat facing each other at the small kitchen table and ate our cereal. I was exhausted and my body ached, but it was hard to feel any sense of achievement in having completed the journey. It was as though there was an invisible wall between Eva and myself, stopping us from connecting with each other properly. I felt very distant from her that night, but she was tired as well and it was very late.

'Are you okay with sleeping on the sofa?' she asked after we had finished eating.

'Yes, that's fine.' I opened my suitcase and began to unpack the items that I would need.

'I'm going to go to bed then.' She hovered in the doorway. 'Will you be all right tonight?'

'Yes, yes, I'll be fine.'

'Well, goodnight then.'

'Goodnight, I look forward to seeing you tomorrow.'

'And you. Goodnight.'

'Goodnight.' I watched as she closed the sitting room door and then heard her moving about in the bathroom. It had been a harrowing day and I was looking forward to finally resting, but I knew that it wouldn't be possible to really relax. So many issues were unresolved, and so many concerns crowded my mind.

Chapter Four

Although, looking back now on those first few days in Germany, I can see that the darkness was already gathering, it seemed at the time to be little more than the grey drabness of a reality that did not shine as brightly as my dreams. I had spent so many hours imagining how wonderful the reunion with Eva would be that the period of readjustment was all the more painful, and sometimes appeared to have no end in sight. On the Sunday and Monday we had taken walks and talked a great deal, but had still been far from our original romance, behaving in many ways more like old friends than lovers. We ate our meals in the little kitchen, and it was in the mornings that I felt the worst, when I would eat a bowl of cereal and stare out into the street below, finding it almost impossible to make conversation and seeing no way through the barrier between us, the day long and frustrating before us. Sometimes we watched a few programmes on television, and all throughout there was a mood of staleness and frustration, as if the best days were already gone.

On the Tuesday matters improved, though not at once. It was the first day that Eva had to attend university and we were preparing to leave the house quite early. I sat on the sofa while she walked to and fro, gathering up the items that she would need for the day. The sun was very bright and shone through the half-drawn curtains, marking a vivid slash of light across the table, and as I let my gaze wander around the room and out to the morning city I realised that I was lonely. Lonely not for a person but rather for a time—lonely for the weeks that Eva and I had been happiest together. Frequently over the past months I had counted the days that had passed since she had left England, and now it occurred to me that I was still counting, still missing those earliest times despite our being together again.

'Tonight or tomorrow night I must visit my mother,' Eva said as she pushed a folder into her bag.'

'Of course. How often do you normally see her?'

'Every two or three days.'

'Don't forget that we're going to meet Jens at lunchtime.' The previous evening I had spoken to Jens on the phone and we had arranged to meet at twelve o'clock. He attended the same university and we planned to have a meal in the canteen.

It didn't take Eva long to pack, and we stepped out into the impatient June heat to catch the bus. The stop was only five minutes' walk from the flat, through the dazzled, sunburnt streets, and the bus took us to the main station where we changed to the university route. It was a half hour trip, away from the city and through a stretch of countryside before arriving at the university town.

'Would you like to attend my lecture?' Eva asked partway through the journey.

'Is it in German?'

'Yes.'

'I won't be able to understand it then.'

'That's nothing to worry about, I don't understand it most of the time.'

'What are the other options?' I asked, noticing a man in a bright yellow outfit cycling in the opposite direction.

'You could go in the library and read, or perhaps wait in a computer room.'

'How long is the lecture?'

'Two hours, but there's a little break in the middle.' She paused for a moment and examined a nail. 'If I were in your position I would go in the library and wait; there are plenty of books in English.'

'You're probably right.'

'And I can come and see you at half-time.'

'Yes.'

'And rescue you when it's over. Then we can go and meet Jens.'

'It should be fine.' It was, I considered, probably for the best that I should not attend the lecture as there was little to be gained from sitting through two hours of monologue which held no meaning for me.

On the route we passed fields of poppies, colour like a great, beautiful sadness at the unceasing flow of time and the inevitability of suffering.

In Flanders fields the poppies blow
Between the crosses, row on row

Poppies, I thought, would still grow here long after Eva and I were dead with all our struggles forgotten. What people would pass here in a hundred years time? What thoughts would float here then?

After reaching the university town we walked to the building that held the library as well as most of the large lecture halls. There was no campus, and the various administrative and academic locations were spread around the area. Eva led the way into the huge library and pointed out where the books written in English were shelved.

'There are quite a few to choose from,' she said, pulling a history of Europe from the shelf and handing it to me. 'How about this one?'

'That'll do to start with. I can always take another if it gets boring.' I put the book down on a table.

'Will you be all right sitting here then?'

'I'll be fine. You sound like a mother leaving her child,' I grinned.

'Well, you seem like a child because you can't speak to anyone very easily.' She laughed and checked the time. 'I'd better go now, I'll be back in about an hour for my break.'

'Have a good time.' As she left the room I felt oddly excited by the thought that I would be alone for an hour and then she would return. Being apart occasionally made meeting again all the more special.

The history of Europe did not appeal to, and I eventually chose a book about early English poetry to read. The second concerned the poem "The Green Knight," written by an unknown author in the late medieval period. As I read the description of the story, picturing the scenes in my mind, it once again seemed that I was lost in time, that somehow beyond the library there was a long vanished world, while out-side church bells rang for a land of six hundred years ago—as if the streets and the people of old Bavaria were stirring in a distant place, but already growing closer. Perhaps, I thought, this was simply because I felt so alien sitting alone, with no anchor to reality. There were so many books around that many of them must hardly ever have been touched. Peering around the shelves at names of authors who I had never heard of, it occurred to me that being in a library is similar to being in a graveyard—as years pass most of the popular writers of their day fade until only a handful of people remember them; each of the thousands of books a massive individual effort that, when stowed with the others, seems unremarkable, a thing to be casually glanced at and then forgotten.

As I continued to read there was no sound other than an occasional cough or crackle as a book was pulled from the shelf or replaced. About a dozen students sat around the wooden tables, immersed in their studies, time passing in shadow between the carpeted floor and the high, brown ceil-ing. Eva returned for ten minutes at her half-time break, and we talked for a little until it was time for her to leave again.

'I don't want to go back,' she said, 'but there are too few people to miss the next half. It would be too obvious.'

When she was gone, I scanned the shelves and eventually settled back down with a book on European folklore. Opening a random page I read an account of how a German village named Bingen-am-Rhein was supposedly visited, in the year 355, by a poltergeist which flung stones and pulled the inhabitants out of their beds. A dark night of countless generations past—a strange feeling entered my chest, to think that the names of towns were so similar then to today, to think that the German culture and language of today had its roots in those dark years. There must be something linking past and present, Eva's descendants would have lived then, perhaps in that very village. Already, seventeen centuries ago, history was moving towards our present position. I imagined the fourth-century village, the wide fields and battered houses, the weathered faces of the peasants. Centuries before Eva was born, yet were I able to travel back in time and watch that ancient world for a day, I would occasionally glance, unknowingly, a man or woman who was a distant relation of hers, who, without understanding, was creating the far-off future. Perhaps, even then, I would sense that future already waiting behind a cracked wall or in the wild, fearsome sky; the centuries turning towards a predestined point. As I glanced over names of other reputedly haunted German places, Darmstadt, Brandenburg, Baden, it seemed that all time was one time, that we could just as easily be in the Dark Ages now, as though I could not quite believe that a time ever existed when Eva was not born. I felt so far from home, and yet it seemed that a part of me had been here since eternity, waiting across the centuries for these moments to arrive, watching the German states arise from the broken tatters of Europe.

I continued to read until I saw Eva walking towards me, smiling.

'How was it?' I asked.

'Terrible.' She looked at her watch. 'Anyway, I'm glad it's over but I've got another lecture in an hour's time.'

'And is that two hours as well?'

'Yes. I don't think that Jens has anything in the afternoon, so maybe you can stay with him. Actually, we're supposed to be meeting him soon, we'd better get going.'

We left the library and walked to the building where the university canteen was housed, surrounded by more lecture halls and seminar rooms. The large entrance lobby was crowded with students, either talking in groups or making their way up a flight of stone stairs.

'That's where the food is,' Eva said, jerking her head in the direction of the stairs.

'Do most people eat in the canteen?'

'A lot do. It's different than English universities, I think.'

'Yes, having a central canteen is a good idea, especially when there's no campus.'

We waited for Jens in the entrance lobby, Eva growing increasingly frustrated with the passing minutes as he failed to arrive.

'I hate it when people are late,' she fumed, 'what's holding him up?'

'It doesn't matter, we've got plenty of time.' I was a little afraid of the harsh tone in her voice which threatened to overflow into anger at any moment.

'If he's not here in five minutes then we'll have to go and eat anyway,' she decided, but at that point Jens arrived, sweeping away all agitation and bringing with him an intensely welcome sense of calm. He was a big man, bustling with energy and enthusiasm, the strength of his entrance enough to reverse all negative feelings.

'Sorry I'm late, how are you, Eva? Hello Dave, it's been a long time, how are you doing?' His arrival brought back memories of our time together in England, of days when we both knew Eva but neither of us knew her very well. For a moment I felt a kind of longing for that carefree existence, empty though it now seemed, before romance had made the world so much more severe.

We spoke for a minute before heading up to the canteen where I found that the routine for receiving food was the same as that which I had practised at school. You took a tray and queued until reaching the row of steaming food containers. There you placed your order and watched the required meal being slapped down onto a plate, before moving along to the till. It was all very simple.

'What are you going to order?' Jens asked as we approached the counter.

'I'm not sure. Have you seen what kinds of food they have?'

'Fish is the main meal.'

'I might have the soup,' Eva said as she peered around the bodies in front to gain a better view.

'Soup sounds good.' I stepped forward as the queue advanced.

'What are you doing this afternoon?' Jens asked.

'I don't know yet. Eva has a two-hour lecture. What are you doing?'

'I'm free for the rest of the day. If you want I can show you around the town.'

'We were hoping you would say that,' Eva smiled as she slowly worked her hands around the tray. 'I don't think Dave could stand two hours worth of lecture.'

When it was our turn to order I chose the soup. It wasn't clear whether or not the serving woman was able to speak English, but I pointed at the bowl of soup and she placed it on the tray, along with a roll of bread and a packet of butter. I gave Jens the money to pay for my meal and then we sat down at small, wooden table with four metal chairs around it. The hall was very busy and there were few spare tables—just enough to accommodate the mass of constantly altering diners. Background conversation was diluted with the clatter and scrape of cutlery, pierced at intervals by the malicious summons of a mobile phone. A thin, eager man—a friend of Jens—joined us and was introduced as Matthias.

'How long are you staying in Germany?' he asked in excellent English.

'I'm going back in ten days.'

'Quite a long stay then.'

'They've been to the festival,' Jens said.

'Oh yes. You have to if you come at this time of year.'

'We met a man who told me that it was a fifth season,' I said, breaking off a piece of bread.

'I suppose it is,' Matthias thought for a moment. 'Did you enjoy the festival?'

'He didn't dance much,' Eva interjected.

'Well, I was tired. I'd been travelling all day.'

'We should all go to the festival together at some point,' Jens suggested, tapping his finger on the table to emphasise the idea.

'That's a good plan, Eva and I were thinking the same thing.'

'Perhaps we could go on Friday night.'

'Saturday would be better for me,' Matthias said, looking up from cutting his fish.

'Very well then, Saturday night. Jens turned to Eva. 'Would that suit you?'

'Yes, we don't have many plans.'

'And perhaps we could go on somewhere afterwards.'

'We can see what happens at the time,' Matthias said with enthusiasm. Even I began to look forward to Saturday a little, thinking that it might not be so bad at the festival when I was less exhausted than on our first visit.

We finished our meals and the party broke up. Eva went off to her lecture after arranging to meet us afterwards, and Matthias said that he had work to do in the library. Jens and I went out into the biting afternoon sun, strolling through the sweating streets while he pointed out interesting sites and we discussed events at my home university. It was a small enough town to have a character of its own, pleasant to walk though with a friend, yet somehow I didn't feel right to have left Eva at university. Perhaps, I thought, there was a little jealousy involved – all those young men in her lectures, everything so awfully hot.

Before long we went into a café for a drink, through low doors and into a spacious room filled with tables, every one of which was unoccupied.

'Not the busiest time of day,' Jens muttered, taking a seat by the window. 'What are you going to drink?'

We both ordered tea from a man who appeared from a room behind the counter. When the drinks arrived they were served in tall glasses which made them seem rather special, as if they were a kind of luxury.

'So,' Jens asked after a pause in the conversation, 'how are things between you and Eva?'

'Not bad,' I replied unconvincingly. Part of me was desperate to explain to Jens the problems that we faced, but it was too personal to talk about in detail.

'You know,' he went on, 'I do not particularly like Eva.'

'I thought you might not. She is quite hard to get on with sometimes.'

'Really, she is no girl for you.'

'You think not?'

'But it is of course your choice.' He sipped his tea. I thought how angry I would have felt if anybody but Jens was holding this conversation with me. Somehow he was different and we were able to talk in a totally rational manner.

'I don't know what's going to happen,' I sighed.

'And she's so much older than you. Does that worry you?'

'Yes, yes of course. But—'

'Go on.'

'I kind of like her being older. I don't know why. It makes it all more special.'

'Well, you mustn't let me influence you.'

'I don't understand this love.'

'Who ever did?'

That was it though, I thought, it was all about love. That was what made it possible to penetrate beneath a person's surface, to join with them on a deeper level of compassion, even to see their faults as something positive and exciting. It occurred to me that I had never told Eva out loud that I loved her. Writing it was just not the same.

'It's inexplicable,' Jens reasoned.

'Absolutely.' I made up my mind to tell Eva that I loved her that evening. The thought of it cheered me considerably.

'By the way, you should come and visit my home sometime during your stay,' Jens said.

'Yes, I want to see where you live.'

'Perhaps you could stay a night or two.'

Maybe.' It seemed a good idea to give Eva some free space at some point, but I didn't want to be apart from her for too long.

'You could come back with me after we go out on Saturday night and we could go somewhere on Sunday.'

'Okay then, I'll see what Eva thinks, but it should be fine.'

'You can stay a few nights if you want.'

'Thanks, I appreciate it. Just I want to be with Eva as much as possible.'

'Yes, of course.'

After finishing our tea we went to wait for Eva outside her lecture hall. When she arrived I explained my plan of spending a day with Jens.

'That's a good idea,' she agreed, 'I've got so much work to do that I need to spend a whole day catching up.'

'So on Saturday night we'll all go to the festival, and Dave can come back with me, then I'll take him back to you on Sunday evening,' Jens clinched it.

'And what are we going to do for the rest of today?' Eva asked, turning to me.

'Do you want to go out tonight?'

'Maybe.'

'I'm going to go home now,' Jens took a step backwards, 'so if we don't meet before then I'll see you on Friday. I'll phone you sometime to arrange the time and place.'

'Okay, goodbye.'

'Bye.'

'Bye.'

In the end, Eva and I went back to her flat for a few hours. My feet were hot and sore when I removed my shoes, and my whole body felt uncomfortable. We sat on the sofa and Eva took a few books from her bag. The room was stretched, cracked with heat and I felt irritable and far, far from my dreams of a return to the romantic days of March.

'These are the poems that I have to study for my English course,' she said, showing me the chapter. I took the heavy book and glanced at the page. The poem I saw was "Dover Beach" by Matthew Arnold.

> *The sea is calm tonight.*
> *The tide is full, the moon lies fair*
> *Upon the straits — on the French coast the light*
> *Gleams and is gone*

Such melodious sadness — it brought a tightness to my throat as I felt Eva sitting beside me. I loved her so much, and the weight of it struck once again at my soul. I could never live without her, yet all my desires seemed to be rotting away.

> *The sea of Faith*
> *Was once, too, at the full, and round earth's shore*
> *Lay like the folds of a bright girdle furled.*
> *But now I only hear*
> *It's melancholy, long, withdrawing roar*

The problem was knowing what to say, and having the courage to say it. I wanted to talk about love, but the time was not right, and she hardly seemed in the mood. I let her continue with her study, while the clock on the shelf continued to count away our time together, every tick like an urgent call to act, and it seemed that the sun had brought a mist down over my brain so that it was impossible to think.

The afternoon creaked along in this manner until later on, in the evening, we decided to visit a bier garten which Eva told me she was particularly fond of.

'We'll have to catch a bus, because it's quite a long way,' she said, checking the time. 'I think I'll put some different clothes on before we leave.'

We had drawn the curtains for the heat, so she changed in the sitting room, stripping off to her under-clothes and dressing in a colourful skirt and blouse that had been draped over a chair. From the sofa, I could hardly avoid watching her undress. Seeing her almost naked brought a rush of that suppressed physical lust through my body—it seemed to confuse everything still further. There were so many different ways that I loved her—the way that made me happy for us just to be together, the way that demanded sex and bodily possession, and the part of me that wanted us to sit on the sofa with our arms around each other, talking about silly things and knowing that our love would continue forever.

We caught the bus and spent half an hour idling through the waking seven o'clock coolness of the city, with every street an almost unperceivable fragment of the entirety. Peering through the jolting window, I was particularly struck by the mixture of old and new that existed in Eva's city. Modern housing, older buildings that must have seen several generations, bridges and barns that could have been hundreds of years old, all intermingled. So strange to think that for a thousand years people had been making their homes here. Although we were quite a distance from the city centre, it was somehow possible to *sense* the medieval fortresses and roadways that formed the hub of the metropolis, as though all the life were radiating from there.

On seeing the bier garten for the first time I was struck by the mood of peace that surrounded it—a large grass area covered with wooden tables, and the food and drink stalls set to one side. It was fairly busy and there was a happy murmur as families, couples and groups of men and women laughed and drunk and rested from the torrents of life. We found a free table and each bought a half litre of beer mixed with flavoured lemonade. The drink was served in tall glasses, larger versions of the tea glasses that I had drunk from earlier, and I was so parched that it was difficult not to gulp it too quickly. As Eva and I talked, I remembered the promise that I had made to myself earlier—to tell her that I loved her. It was impossible to know how to go about saying such a thing, so as the minutes passed I decided to begin and hope for the best.

'Eva?' My heart was pounding.

'Yes?'

'There's, err, there's something that I want to tell you.' She made no reply, so I continued. 'It's actually quite a hard thing to say.'

Before I could go any further, she stood up.

'I just have to go to the toilets. I'll be back in a minute.'

'No, don't go now, I have to talk to you for a bit.'

'I'll be back in a minute.'

'Wait—damn.' She walked off towards the toilet building and left me horribly frustrated, wondering whether she had guessed what I was going to say and didn't want to hear it, or whether it was simply bad luck. Either way, as she returned I realised that the moment had passed and there was no way that I could try again that evening.

This was the first point at which I absolutely despaired for our future. There seemed to be nothing left but the hopelessness of memory, the peculiar relief of a battle lost. But, as the evening continued beneath the melody of bird song mixed with the chink and clank of glasses, we both relaxed, and suddenly the invisible wall that I had felt so keenly between us was weakening. I put my arm around her waist and she took my hand and held it very tightly, so that it felt as though we were finally making up for an argument that had raged in our minds but had never found expression in words.

'I've missed you,' I said quietly. 'You wouldn't believe how much I've missed you.'

'Of course we miss each other,' she murmured, smoothing her hair with her free hand. 'It won't ever be easy.'

We sat holding each other for a long time beneath the warm evening sky. The world was a happy place, and there was new hope as the trees shivered to the whisper of descending night, soft and romantic. Love, I thought, had a force that would make itself felt whether it was spoken of or not. Perhaps some things didn't need to be said out loud.

The bus that we caught back home that night was full of people who had been to the festival. Once again the vehicle was filled with drunken shouting and laughter, but it was no longer aggressive—everybody was simply having a good time with no thoughts of violence. The passengers urged the driver to overtake a slow moving truck and, when he eventually did, a great roar of celebration went up. For the first time since my arrival I began to really look forward to the coming days, even though the next few would be largely taken up by trips to the university. We walked home from the bus stop and the city was restful around us, growing almost homely beneath the stars and the kind moon.

Chapter Five

The bleeping of my watch alarm woke me and I lifted myself from the sofa, standing for a moment at the edge of the room as its now familiar smell crept through my mind, easing me back into the present. Crossing to the window I opened one curtain, allowing the bright Saturday morning to rush into the room. It was another red-hot day, and I was growing weary of the heat. Every day upon waking it was the same—rising from the sofa with a slight headache, to be greeted by a sun that was already soaring in the sky and had long before made the world outside sticky and uncomfortable.

In the half-week that had passed since our trip to the bier garten, Eva and I had continued our confused, often obstructed relationship. She was distant in her emotions for much of the time so that I began to realise how little I really knew about her, how slight my understanding was of the ways she thought and reasoned. Even when we were close enough to hold each other and speak words that meant 'I love you' in all but form, she would still seem frustrated with a hopeless anxiety, as though afraid or hindered by some deep feeling of guilt.

Twice she had gone to visit her mother and, left alone in the flat, I was more of an alien than ever, feeling as though I was hiding from the authorities like a religious convict. When I walked, persecution seemed to stalk beside me, not caused by a particular person or institution but rather by our own failings and the complex situation. Often I wondered whether I was fooling myself with thoughts of our future, as the problems of age and distance and language boiled continuously in my imagination; but then there were happy moments as well, times when we both relaxed to feel the warmth of being together, and then it seemed that everything would work itself out in the end.

'Good morning.' Eva had entered the room silently and I jumped, as though caught in the act of explaining her defects to a friend. As ever, upon seeing her for the first time in a day I was both thrilled and saddened by the beauty of her body and her movements, as if some great treasure stood before me that was doomed to crumble into dust, leaving a vast hollowness in its place.

'Hello darling, did you sleep well?'

'Not badly.' She joined me at the window and we gazed without speaking over the small part of the city that was visible. There were more flats obstructing our view, tall and lifeless against the breathing sky.

'It would be nice to go for a walk later on,' she said eventually. 'We have to phone Jens as well.'

'Yes, I'm looking forward to tonight,' I agreed half truthfully, wishing that we were all meeting up for a private party instead of going out into the frightening world.

We called Jens a little later and arranged to meet at eight o'clock in a square near the entrance to the festival. Before lunchtime Eva sat at the living room table with her books and immersed herself in university work, while I lay, half dozing on the sofa, occasionally reading a few lines of an English language book that she had given me. After eating a meal of pasta and sauce we set out on the proposed stroll.

After a week in residence I still had no idea of my way around the city, recognising only vaguely the streets that we passed on our regular trips to the bus stop. Now we turned left instead of right at the front door, quickly heading down a road that was entirely new to me. There were tall, white buildings all along its length in a style that would have been fresh and modern fifty years earlier, but was now as tired as the grey stones of the aged path. After ten minutes we came to the top of a rise where the road ended and, spread out below us, was a huge area of grass and parkland laying on either side of a wide river.

'It's nice to walk down there,' Eva pointed at a gravel path which led down to the park. 'On a hot day it's the best place to be.'

We descended the path until reaching a tarmac road that ran along the length of the river. There was one section for pedestrians and one for cyclists, and every minute or so a bicycle would crash past, its rider steaming onwards and out of our view and our lives within an instant. And as we walked along the edge of the water with all humanity shimmering around us – the boys playing on the old, concrete bridge, the families taking air, the detached, basking hiker – it still seemed to be all an illusion, a subtle trick of the subconscious. I could smell the water, could feel a slight breeze against my cheek and hear birds rustling in the trees – so many images and smells were familiar that it could have been any normal day from my past, yet this made it all the stranger. The overriding impression was of unreality; I could not quite believe that I was walking with Eva by a German river. Somehow the truth was beyond my imagination, for how could these people, this path, this land exist? How was it that I could anticipate every shadow, every random thought, remaining with me forever, whether for the better or the worse?

'You see there?' Eva gestured to the boys on the bride. 'My father used to play there when he was young.'

'Yes, yes of course. It must be interesting to have a family who have always lived here.' I wondered what the correct attitude was at this moment, whether she was saddened by the thought of her dead father. It was a subject that we never discussed, and I had no idea of when he had died; it could have been ten years before or within the last twelve months.

'If you had been a boy here you probably would have played there also,' she continued, 'most children from around here go there at times.' I looked at the bridge again but it was such a bleak object that associating it with childhood caused me to shiver.

After three-quarters of an hour we reached a point where the path forked, and took the route that led into open country-side. The city limits had been passed and we now moved along its western edge, down footpaths which led through farm-land, frequently passing large groups of hikers with deter-mined grimaces. The fields were yellow and brown, again like a memory of walks taken in other summers and other lands.

'I used to come here a lot,' Eva said at length. 'About five years ago I was always down this way.'

'It's funny that you can walk from the edge of the city and be here within an hour.' I peered down the track which contin-ued into the horizon until it was lost among trees. 'How far are we planning to go?'

'If we carry on in this direction we'll eventually reach a little town, though I'm not sure how long it'll take us to get there. It may not leave us in good shape for tonight's party.'

We continued to walk for over an hour, through balmy countryside with the spirit of civilised nature rustling in the air amidst the chatter of birds and occasional whisper of breeze. After a long while we reached the town, and by that time we were both parched, my throat cracked and dry like the road-side mud.

'We should find somewhere to get a drink,' I suggested, 'before we die of dehydration.'

'I was thinking the same; there must be a pub or a bier garten nearby in a town of this size. The trouble is I don't really know this area at all.'

The road that we were following was long and dusty with houses stretching away over a distant rise. It looked as though it could go on forever. We turned down a side path but it led us further into an estate that was all residential and held nothing of greater value to us than a corner store that was closed. My head was aching with the lack of fluid and it felt as though we were wandering through a desert, going around in circles in a hopeless quest for water.

'I'll ask these people where we can get a drink,' Eva said, glancing up the road to where a middle-aged couple were approaching us. She held a brief conversation with them and the couple smiled and pointed so it was obvious that they were giving directions. Listening to them all talking in a language that I could not understand was a curiously lonely experience, as though I did not quite exist, standing and listening on the edge of that pavement without knowing what was being said. I thought for a moment about speech—about how the German language has so many different dialects, especially Franconia, up in the north of Bavaria where it is almost a different language altogether. All these ancient nations, now bound up into one modern state, but with so much of their own history and culture that they seem in many ways quite independent of one another.

Following the directions we found a bier garten, small but delightful with tables among ornamental trees and water features so that it felt like a garden of paradise, a place that is visited in daydreams. A woman came to the table to take our order and when the drinks arrived I felt as though I could not have waited another minute. As the first sip of liquid touched my throat I felt a sharp, momentary pain behind my forehead and a swirling giddiness that passed in an instant. Again, we drank beer mixed with flavoured lemonade, its refreshing, pleasant taste one which I knew would, with a touch of sadness, remain with me always, drawing me back to these sunbound, unreal moments whenever the flavour returned to my mind.

'I wonder how we should get home again,' Eva said, tapping the side of her glass. 'Do you want to walk any more?'

'If there a bus route back?'

'There's a train that would take us near my flat. I think it passes through the station here quite regularly.'

'That's a good idea then, it'll save us getting too exhausted.' For the second time in the day I was suddenly struck by the powerful, somehow tragic, sense of physical attraction that I felt for Eva. Sitting on the bench she was divine, wearing a pair of red shorts instead or her usual long, light skirt, and all that confusing, pulsating desire was mixed up with a deep, inexplicable dread.

'Tomorrow I must go and see my mother again,' she said, smiling. 'She said that I was looking tired the other day so I told her that it was because I had been working late at the university. It's fun in a way, making up excuses.'

'It's a shame you have to lie so much.'

'It is.' She couldn't understand how it hurt me when she pretended to her family that I didn't exist. There seemed to be little point in arguing about it. 'My only fear,' she continued, 'is that one day my mother's going to suddenly pop in to the flat, but she doesn't go out anymore, so it's very unlikely.'

'I would like it if she did pop in, then you wouldn't have to lie.' I said, unable to restrain myself from making the point.

'*You* don't have to lie though.'

In a way, I thought, it was all a lie. I didn't really care whether Eva told her mother the truth or not, it was simply that if her family were aware of our relationship then it would make it official, and therefore more stable.

'What are you going to do with Jens tomorrow?' she asked.

'I have no idea. I imagine that he'll think of something. I'll miss you a bit.'

'Yes.' She smiled as though trying to think of the correct reply, and failing to find it, she stared down into her glass.

It was peaceful in the garden but I found it hard to relax with thoughts of the forthcoming evening. After finishing our drinks we walked up to the old train station for the journey back to the city and our night's adventures.

We waited for Jens in the main square of the university town. It was eight o'clock and busy with people on their way to the festival, but the crowds were not as frightening as they had been on my first visit. There was more the atmosphere of a fairground than a nightclub and no drunken cries yet tore though the calm. After we had waited for ten minutes, Jens and Matthias arrived with another man of about twenty-five years and two women of a similar age. They were all introduced but I forgot their names instantly.

'We're all going to the festival together then,' Jens smiled as we began walking. 'It's a multinational event.'

'Which tent are we going to?' I asked. 'Are we going to dance on tables at all?'

'Perhaps,' he looked at me as though it were a surprising question. 'Perhaps we will.'

'In many ways I'd rather just sit somewhere, if that's not too boring.' He made no reply, so I walked next to Eva, watching as the group shifted and changed. Sometimes Jens spoke with Matthias and sometimes he chatted with the two girls or the other man, but all the while I was aware of the patter of our shoes against the concrete that was drawing us towards a fear that seemed to be waiting ahead.

We reached the festival, the fairground air still evident along the main path in a wash of colourful stalls selling food, drink and various gifts under a covering of bright, brisk music and the dreamland of early evening. Most powerful of all were the smells — that mixture of dry grass and lemonade and pretzels, fusing together into the spirit of the moment.

'You should buy a t-shirt,' Eva suggested, 'to prove to people that you've been here.'

'Yes, a t-shirt is vital on these occasions,' Jens agreed.

I glanced at the shirts for sale. Most of them were tattooed with a picture of a beer mug and a few words affirming the wearer's presence at the festival. They were fine to look at but rather expensive, and hardly seemed important.

'I'll probably buy one later on in the week,' I lied. 'Maybe we'll come down in the day sometime.'

For one hour we pocked around the stalls, one of our group occasionally making a purchase. Matthias tried his skill at a steady hand game but was unable to move the ring over a quarter of the way around the circuit without setting off the alarm.

'You have a go now,' Eva urged me.

'Are you sure you don't want a go?'

'No, go on.'

'Okay then.' I handed the attendant a one-mark coin and began to inch the metal ring around its path. Slowly, but trying and keep it smooth, trying to maintain a rhythm—further now than Matthias had reached—no, the buzzer sounded, it was over. I turned back, smiling.

'It was a good try,' one of the girls said, addressing me for the first time.

'You have a go now,' I told Jens.

'No, no,' he replied, 'I do not think that my hands are as steady as they once were.'

'Shall we buy a drink?' Matthias asked.

'We might as well.' I was looking forward to a drink, so long as we didn't have to dance. Jens spoke to the man and the two girls in German for a while, before announcing that we were going to buy some beer.

'That is, after all, what we have come for,' he said, leading the way towards a tent.

It was peaceful inside, despite being busy, and we bought drinks from a counter that was really a collection of wooden tables set out in a row. Afterwards, we went to sit outside where rows of picnic benches were sparsely occupied at the edge of a wooded area. The smells of the fading day and the secret trees lent an enchanted air to the entire scene. Bavarian folk music played from a nearby tent, like a mysterious dream to my mind—I felt like I was part of a folk-tale.

'This is fine,' Matthias said, taking a gulp of his beer.

'Dave, what's it like to have finished the year at university?' Jens asked.

'It's good,' I replied with no idea as to what would be an appropriate answer. 'I've got fifteen weeks holiday altogether for the summer. It'll be a bit of a shock when I have to get a job—having twenty days leave a year instead of over a hundred.

'We work a lot more at German universities,' Jens grinned.

'Yes, but you don't have steady hands.' A light breeze blew across my face and I wished that we didn't have to move elsewhere. The evening would be very pleasant if we could stay until late by the quiet of the trees and then go safely home. Minutes passed quickly, the conversation swinging from subject to subject while my inner thoughts rushed between dazed hopes and concerns. I took Eva's hand and she let me hold it, but only with a curious lack of warmth, as though her fingers were making an invisible protest against our love.

Eventually a man came to the table and spoke a few words with Matthias.

'He says that we're not supposed to be sitting here because this area's for people with a different brand of beer,' Matthias explained.

'Really?'

'Yes, they do that sometimes.'

We left the table, and the two girls went off alone, Jens explaining that they were going to meet some other people. The rest of us walked to another tent, this one more boisterous, but to my relief we didn't try and find a table in the middle of the fray but stood at the back where it was possible to talk, away from the flashing crack of beer mugs and scream of voices. Jens and Matthias began to talk in earnest, leaving me wishing that I could think of something interesting to say to Eva. I had run out of conversation and was so tired that it was difficult not to yawn. It seemed that my body and soul were being fast worn down by the exhausting days and restless nights. Eva began talking with the other man, whose name I had forgotten, and for a moment I felt the cut of jealousy because she was speaking with somebody else where I had failed to amuse her.

For a few minutes I did nothing but glance around the tent, noting once again the mud of the floor, the clamour of music and the clattering thoughts of hundreds of minds. Then, returning my gaze to our group, I began to wonder what Eva and the man were talking about, and suddenly it was obvious that my earlier jealousy had not been without foundation. Something about the man's mannerisms, about the predatory glint in his eyes, made it clear that he was interested in Eva in more than a conversational manner. The truth collapsed through my nervous system, weakening my legs and pulling at the heart.

'Where are we planning on going later on tonight?' I asked, desperate to enter the conversation but with no idea as to what to say.

'We'll see in a bit,' Eva replied, turning briefly towards me. My soul was being stretched in all directions. The man was interested in Eva; the pot of fear was boiling over. *Look at them talking*, I thought. *Look at her smiling at what he says, they're probably just talking about their lives, but it's evident what he wants. He must be in his mid-twenties, much more likely a boyfriend than you. When people see them now they must think that they're dating and you're just a friend or a brother.*

'We're thinking about moving to a nightclub soon,' Jens said, draining the remnants from his mug.

'Great.' I had no desire to go to a nightclub, but perhaps when we began to walk it would break the spell that was blocking me emotionally from Eva.

'Let us go forth,' Matthias laughed, leading the way out of the tent and back down the main path into the town. Against the now menacing atmosphere of the streets swarming with drunks I was nearly overcome by the chaos in my mind. I kept step next to Eva, but still the man would make the occasional comment that would make her laugh, and I could not think of a single thing to say.

'This club is my favourite in the area,' Jens was saying. 'In fact it's the first ever nightclub that I visited, when I was seventeen.'

'You wouldn't be able to do that now,' Matthias joined. 'They check to make sure you're over eighteen if they think you're too young.'

I was hardly listening. *Can't this man see what he's doing? Why can't he leave us alone? What if when I'm gone away they* — *No, don't torture yourself like this.*

We arrived at the nightclub, paying the entrance fee and moving down a wide, dull corridor to one of the dance floors. It was not as busy as I had imagined it would be, there was plenty of space, and it could have been enjoyable had it not been for the man, still glancing at Eva, terrifying me with the thought that at any moment he might ask her to dance with him.

The music was loud but pleasant, though the lights steamed insecurity over the floor. A lot of men must see Eva as an easy target, I thought, what with the clothes she wore and her good looks. It was more than that though, it was something about the way she acted, the way she smiled at everyone and laughed so much. It wasn't her fault, but certain men could easily misunderstand her.

After a while Jens told me that we were going to move to a different part of the room, and the whole preceding day focused down into a few heady moments. As we eased our way across the sparsely inhabited floor, the man moved his arm to encircle Eva's waist. Without making a conscious decision to act I threw out my hand and pushed his arm firmly away, then continued walking by Eva's side without looking back. When we arrived at the new area and began to dance again the entire mood had changed; the threat was over, and the man kept a distance away from us.

Looking across at him a few minutes later, he seemed actually upset. I felt almost guilty, wondering whether I had hurt his feelings or overreacted—but no, he had been trying to upset me in the first place.

As the evening continued the club grew busier, and with every new group pushing in near us it became less friendly. After an hour the other man left, sullenly shaking my hand before departing. I felt no satisfaction at having faced down the situation, only pain that it had developed in the first place. With his departure, however, a new phase of agony began. More and more bodies shoved their way onto the floor, the space decreasing beneath the terrible, burning lights and leering music. It was only a matter of time before something awful happened; aggression was clotting the atmosphere, rising from the very foundations of the night. A man winked at Eva and my heart turned over. I checked my watch: half past twelve, and we might not leave until three. There was no chance of surviving for over two hours, it was too long to even contemplate, too dangerous to think about. There was nothing to do but endure, live through each minute and let time melt away on its own. Another group of men moved closer to us and several of them cast glances in our direction. Impulsively I took hold of both of Eva's hands, and she pulled me towards her so that we were dancing very close with our bodies pressed against each other. It was a revelation that she wanted to dance in this way; that she wanted to be close to me at all. Somehow, throughout the preceding hours, I had convinced myself that I had failed, at least in a physical sense, to hold her interest.

For the rest of the night we danced together most of the time, splitting apart only occasionally. The feel of her body made me want to shout out how much I loved her, and, as the occasional flash of light lit every line of her face, I realised just how much attracted I was to her age. She was perfect in her late-twenties, the difference in years between us made everything more special, more exciting and loving. My mind was awash with the beauty and the terror of the situation. *She does love you, but you'll only be together for another week. It'll be okay because you can return soon, perhaps in a month or so – but there are so many other men who find her attractive, the man at the station, the man from tonight. Yes, but she loves you; she's not a child who has to be watched, she's not your property, there has to be some trust between the two of you. But even the knowledge that another man might try to chat her up is painful; but it doesn't matter, you trust each other, don't you?*

As time moved slowly onwards the terror began to outweigh the beauty. I was so exhausted that I could hardly dance; the room was crowded so that people were always jostling each other and violence seemed very near. I could almost feel myself physically shrinking, other clubbers towering above me, reeking with hostility. I began to cling to Eva more for protection than fondness, wondering how much longer I could stand the chocking conditions, as though my brain was about to explode with tension. I felt thin and pathetic; I wondered whether Eva was disappointed with me, whether I was a failure for not enjoying myself.

'How long do you want to stay?' I shouted in Eva's ear.

'We'll have to leave when Jens does,' she replied. We carried on dancing. Another big man reeled towards us and shouted something before turning back to his friends. He had a long, stupid-looking face and was clearly very drunk. I could feel panic rising within me, wanting to run out of the place and never return. I had no idea what the man had shouted, but he was dancing only a few paces away, and he could return at any time. If he was drunk enough he might try and start trouble, or grab hold of Eva, or something worse. I felt sick with worry, desperately hoping that he wouldn't approach us again. The music continued to thump down and everything was confusion—part of my mind was shrieking that I had to get out, to escape before it was too late, but I couldn't do that. Somehow we carried on dancing and time dragged on.

Finally, after an infinity of raging, leering fear, Jens shouted into my ear that it was time to leave.

'We should get home soon,' he continued, 'it's closing time in a few minutes.'

With a huge rush of relief I followed the others back through the room and out of the building. It was noisy outside, crowds still on their way to and from clubs, but it was also wonderfully cool, and the fresh air reopened parts of my mind that had earlier ceased to function. It was like waking from a fraught dream. Then there was the sound of a bottle smashing nearby, and I realised that the evening was still not over. I wanted to leave as soon as possible.

'So, Dave is coming with me,' Jens said as the four of us stood on the pavement.

'Are you okay to get home?' I asked Eva.

'Yes, the bus is leaving soon.'

'Shall we wait with you?'

'No, don't worry. I often do this trip at night.'

'All right then. I'll see you tomorrow.'

'Yes, have a good day.' She walked away towards the bus stop. I wished that we had been able to say goodbye properly, it seemed such an anticlimax just saying goodnight, but it was very late.

'We shall walk home,' Jens informed me. 'It'll take half an hour. Matthias lives in the same village.'

'Ah, so we can all walk together.'

We left the town, down the main road and out onto a tarmac lane that ran through countryside. It was a great relief to escape from the drunken yells and police sirens of the dangerous night, yet I was still confused. It had been one of the worst evenings of my life, but Eva and I had survived it together. The future was no clearer now than it had been before, though at least it held new hopes as well as new anxieties. As we continued to walk, tiredness replaced all other feelings. By the time we reached Jens's village, all that mattered was a bed and rest.

Chapter Six

Throughout the entire walk home I was aware of a lack of sensation in my legs and a feeling that my feet were not touching the ground. The three of us must have resembled a group of battered soldiers retuning from war.

'I shall not be rising early tomorrow,' Matthias yawned as we entered the village.

'Matthias leaves us here,' Jens informed me, 'but we shall see him again tomorrow.'

'Goodnight then.'

'Goodnight.' He turned away down a street. We continued to walk.

'It's very peaceful here,' I noted.

'Yes, it's a good place to live.'

The dark roads were tranquil, very different to the town that we had left behind. I wondered whether Eva had reached home, what she was doing there. It was strange to be apart, not to know each other's exact movements, the smiles and frowns and idleness of an evening.

'What time shall we get up tomorrow?' Jens asked.

'What time do you think?'

'How about eleven o'clock? That would give us nearly eight hours from now.'

'That's fine.'

'This is my house,' he said, turning down the path of a tall, comfortable building, nestling among several other homes of similar appearance; welcoming in the early morning darkness, seeming to lead into a safe retreat from the friction of the world without. Jens found the key and led the way inside. Again, the inexplicable smell of an unfamiliar home—the odour of generations of living—was the overriding sensation that touched me upon entering. We passed though a small entrance hall, lined on both sides with coats and shoes, and into a large kitchen with a table in the middle of the floor.

'This is a nice place,' I said, meaning it. There was a relaxingly modern feel to the room which contained such gleaming white utensils as a coffee machine and a bread maker. It felt as though it had been designed with modest well-being in mind, taking advantage of technology without allowing it to become the master.

'Thank you, I like it as well. Would you like to eat something?'

'That'd be great.' I was surprised by how hungry I suddenly felt; for a while it replaced weariness as the dominant sentiment of my body. Jens went to a cupboard, taking out a brown paper packet, which contained a loaf of already cut bread, then to the fridge for a block of butter and two cheeses. We ate almost in silence; the bread was delicious with the strong cheese, and as the food returned life and warmth to my body it also induced an overpowering tiredness until I felt that I would fall asleep at the table before long.

'What are we going to do tomorrow?' I asked.

'We shall meet Matthias again, and also his girlfriend, and we may go swimming.'

'Swimming?'

'Yes, there's a lake near here that's lovely to swim in.'

'So, outdoors then?' I thought it sounded cold and possibly embarrassing. It had been a long time since I had last taken a swim.

'It'll be fine, so long as the weather is good. Can you ride a bicycle?'

'I used to ride a little, but I haven't tried for ages.'

'We'll probably cycle there you see.'

'It could be very interesting, cycling and swimming in the same day. I'm not very good at either. Also, I don't have any swimming trunks.' I nodded my head towards my small luggage bag, containing just the essentials for an overnight stay.

'That's no problem, I can lend you anything you need; we must have some trunks that'll fit you.' He smiled with hearty enthusiasm in his eyes. It was difficult not to be excited about a project when Jens had his heart set on it.

'I'm really tired,' I said after we had finished eating, 'perhaps we should turn in for the night.'

'Very well, it is a good idea. Tomorrow you shall meet my parents.'

'Yes, I look forward to it. Do your parent speak English at all?'

'No, but I don't think that it will be a problem.'

'Of course not.'

'Have you learnt much German?'

'No, no, I'm afraid not. I've tried quite a bit,' I lied, 'but it's not easy.'

'You should try for Eva's sake. Maybe I can teach you something about the language.'

'That'd be good.'

'For the moment though we should go to bed.' We rose up and he led the way to the staircase and up two flights of still and softly carpeted stairs. 'The room is quite pleasant,' he whispered as we climbed.

'I'm sure it'll be great. I just need somewhere to sleep.'

He opened a door and stepped through. Following him, I entered a spacious, flowing room, the sort that could used be used to live in as well as sleep in. A washbasin stood in the corner and several comfy chairs were dotted around, the scene bringing to mind images of cosy, wet afternoons, and early mornings of hopeful energy.

'It's wonderful,' I said. 'Very big.'

'Thank you. My room is rather smaller.'

'Why don't you move up here?'

'I like my room.'

'Of course.'

'So, we shall rise at eleven o'clock,' he said, glancing at his watch.

'Yes, that should be fine.'

'Goodnight then,' he turned towards the doorway.

'Goodnight.' As soon as the door was closed I experienced a great sense of well-being. Throughout the entire week
the only instances where I had gained any privacy were when
left alone in Eva's living room, but then there was always a
slight feeling of unease, of guilt. In the guest bedroom at Jens's
house I was, for the first time since leaving home, able to really
relax. I sat on the bed and slowly took my pyjamas from my
bag, examining the walls more closely as I did so. There was a
shelf at the far edge, upon which were various items that had
obviously been collected over a considerable period of time;
beer jugs displaying pictures of different festivals, little models
of unfamiliar figures, several plates tattooed with a scene and a
motto. On the wall near the washbasin there were framed
sketches of people, mainly just the heads. Lying in bed I idly
wondered how long ago the sketches had been made, what the
people depicted in them now looked like. For a while my mind
turned over the events of the day, trying to come to terms with
my current position, considering what the next day would
bring, but I was exhausted and fell asleep within minutes.

Throughout the morning, as I passed between light slumber
and even lighter consciousness, the sound of heavy church
bells echoed through the room. Checking my watch, which I
had placed on the bedside table, I found that I was falling
asleep for roughly thirty-minute intervals. Eight o'clock, half
past, quarter past nine, ten minutes to ten. The hour of eleven
crept closer, and still I felt in no way inclined to give up my fit-
ful dozing or the comfort of the bed. The dreams that I experienced in each burst of sleep were intense but difficult to
remember; and when my watch alarm broke up the final
dream I awoke with no recollection of it at all besides a certainty that it had concerned my family at home. My intention
had been to rise as soon as the alarm sounded at a quarter to
eleven, but somehow my body refused to obey, and by the

time Jens knocked on the door at five past the hour, I had only just begun to wash myself.

'Are you nearly ready?' he called through the door.

'Almost. I'll be about ten minutes.'

In the end it took me fifteen. Looking out of the window before going downstairs I was moved by the view, sweeping down through the village and out into rolling countryside of piercing summer green and yellow. There was a great life out there, some endless pastoral being, hidden between the glare of the sun and buzz of insects in the long field grass.

'We shall probably be eating at midday, if that's convenient.' Jens said, arriving at the top of the stairs as I stepped out of the door.

'Great, that's fine. What time did you get up?'

'Not long ago. How are you feeling?'

'Not so bad.'

'You might as well come downstairs.' He led the way downward. 'It's a beautiful day.'

'Yes, I saw from the window. Another hot one.'

We reached the ground floor and walked through to the kitchen, where Jens's parents were sitting. They rose to meet us as we entered, his father grinning and shaking my hand with a joviality that swelled to contain the entire room. He was a large man, very much an older version of his son, nearing sixty years; his face pinched with the lines of a busy life. His wife was tall and slim, perhaps five or ten years younger than her husband, with eyes that were soft and understanding.

The father spoke to me in German and, although I could not recognise exactly what he was saying, somehow the situation and his manner of dialogue enabled me to understand the drift of his meaning—the usual greetings to a stranger, accompanied by such movement of the eyes as to almost create a universal language in itself. By smiling and nodding I felt that we were able to communicate to a fairly successful degree.

'My mother says that we shall eat in ten minutes,' Jens informed me. 'Will that be acceptable?'

'Yes, absolutely. I'm quite hungry.' We withdrew into the hallway, and Jens showed me the lounge, containing a television set and two sofas. There was a welcome sense of family about the entire house, refreshing to feel. After a few minutes we went through to the dining room to eat. I had assumed that we would sit at the kitchen table, but there was a separate room with a large table, covered by a white cloth on which stood various bowls filled with meat and vegetables. Around the walls were wooden shelves holding books and ornaments, similar to those in my temporary room.

It was a comfortable meal, and we helped ourselves to the food while an occasional car rumbled down the gentle road beyond the window.

'My father asks whether you can speak German,' Jens told me as he reached for more salad.

'Not really, I'm afraid,' I shook my head awkwardly, feeling the heat of the slightly spicy meat on my tongue. The father laughed and spoke quickly, also shaking his head.

'My father says that he cannot speak English,' Jens translated; this evidently intended to neutralise my embarrassment. I felt very happy and relaxed. Sunday seemed to have made its presence felt everywhere, and the whole world was calm.

After the meal, Jens and I went into the garden and sat on a bench just outside the door. It was a fine garden, large enough to enjoy, I imagined, without having to spend too much time looking after it; the colours and faint scent of the border flowers making me wish that we did not have to go out anywhere but could remain at ease beneath the gentle skies until evening. The air was alive with the drone of insects, hurrying in seemingly aimless pattern on their endless quest for survival.

'This is a special place,' I said, 'yet at the same time it could be anywhere.'

'How do you mean?' Jens asked, reclining further so that he was almost lying down.

'I mean that if you close your eyes and just listen to the summer you can imagine that we're in any peaceful garden.' I thought about the previous week, of how many times I had walked with Eva through the sunny university grounds; students sprawled around on the dry grass, asleep or with drinks and magazines. We could have been at any university in the world and seen the same relaxed bodies before us, yet such perfect, dreamy scenes did not seem real. I could not relate my inner turmoil to the apparent bliss around us, could hardly believe that I was not about to awaken and find myself years in the future, an old man regretting his dreams of the vanished past. In those moments I had longed to hold Eva very close, to stop her from vanishing back into the fantasy that had created us.

'Matthias will be arriving soon,' Jens said at length. 'I should find you some swimming trunks.'

'Is there a place to get changed there?'

'Yes, don't worry about that.'

He went into the house, presently returning with a towel and pair of trunks.

'Will these suit you?'

'I'm sure they'll be fine. I'd better just go and try them on.' I climbed the stairs back up to my room and changed into the trunks to make sure they fitted. It was cool in the room and I felt a slight thrill of nervous excitement while thinking of the coming trip. It was a tiny adventure, cycling and swimming, but it was of the kind that might be enjoyable. After changing back into my clothes I packed the towel and trunks into my bag and went back downstairs, out into the garden where Jens was waiting.

'They should be here soon,' he said, tapping a finger on the bench and laughing. 'Not that there's much of a hurry.'

After a few minutes a gate at the side of the house opened and Matthias wheeled a bicycle into the garden. A young woman whom I assumed to be his girlfriend followed him. She seemed friendly, smiling a lot, and I felt a certain sense of relief—I had been worried that Jens's friend from the previous night, who had caused me so much worry about Eva, might have joined us on the trip. However, it seemed that it would be just the four of us. Jens's parents were in the garden and began a conversation with the newcomers while Jens led me to a wooden shed in one corner of the garden.

'You can use this great machine,' he said, opening the unlocked door and pulling out a bicycle that seemed to be in good condition. 'I'm afraid that it hasn't been used much recently.'

'Oh, I've seen a lot worse,' I laughed. 'Some of my friends have bikes that are more rust that metal.' I wheeled it out to where the others were standing.

'Jens, tell your parents that this is my first attempt at riding a bike for about ten years.' On translation this announcement caused general merriment, a wave of friendly laughter and jovial comments washed over the group; but Jens's mother, having a slightly concerned look in her eye, made sure that I knew how to brake by showing me the relevant handle. Then we said goodbye to the parents and wheeled the cycles out into the front garden and onto the road.

'This could be amusing,' I informed the company. In fact even mounting the bike was a challenge; Matthias and his girlfriend set off up the road while Jens waited for me. The first time I tried to set off I began to lean at once and had to put my foot on the ground to avoid falling off, but on the second attempt I succeeded in staying upright and began to wobble slowly down the road.

It took us about forty minutes to reach the lake. For the first section of the journey, down the village road, I was obliged to stop at regular intervals in order to regain my balance. When we passed into the country lanes the rhythm became more comfortable, but the going was still very slow. Every now and then we caught up with Matthias and his girlfriend who had stopped to wait for us, and then, as we drew level, watched them shoot off out of sight within a minute.

Despite my lack of cycling ability, it was a pleasant trip. The fields that we crawled though were restful yet full of hidden life, and the few other cyclists that we passed all looked happy, glimmering past us in an instant, sometimes with a brief word of greeting.

'We're almost there now,' Jens told me as we reached a point where the road cut through a group of trees. And indeed, a minute later we arrived at the lake. It was a glittering expanse of enticing blueness, sunbathers spread around its edges with various bolder groups immersed up to their waists in the lapping water. There were trees sparsely dotted about, their leaves silent, sleeping yet listening, serving to increase the mood of the place, the sense of nature and harmony.

On one side of the path there was a brick building containing a shop, a bar, and a few cubicles for changing. Here there was also a place to lock cycles, and we walked over to where Matthias was waiting with his girlfriend.

'Well done. Did you enjoy the ride?' he asked.

'It was interesting.'

'What more can you ask for?' the girlfriend laughed.

We secured our bikes before heading into the building to change, through a wooden door and into a corridor with little, brown cubicles on either side. There was a strange, musty air in the block, somehow exciting — the last act before descending to the chill without. Two minutes later we all met again outside.

'Are you not swimming?' Jens asked Matthias's girlfriend.

'No,' she laughed. 'I shall sit in the sun and watch you. And I can guard your clothes.'

'That's a good idea. It would not be so funny if we had to cycle home dressed as we are.'

'It might be quite funny.' She led the way to the water's edge, into a space between two groups of sunbathers, and spread out a sheet on the dry ground. There was a natural slope to the lake nearby, and Jens headed towards it first, entering the water slowly, painfully, yet moving constantly deeper. Then, with a great splash, he immersed himself completely up to the head.

'Come on,' he cried, his voice a rather higher pitch than normal, 'it's great.'

I stood at the top of the slope, pondering for a moment the warmth of the sun on my skin and the feel of the sandy, dry mud beneath my toes. A tree root stuck out from the bank and I used this to support myself, edging down the bank in a few seconds and experiencing the first sting of the water. It was not as cold as I had imagined it might be, painful against the feet for a moment before neutralising. Now I began to move further in, the gradient falling away rapidly, Jens grinning from nearby, the lake stabbing at me with each step I took as a new part of my body was exposed to it. The time had arrived for the plunge. With an odd sense of pleasure I allowed myself to fall back into the water, its icy arms seizing me in a tight grasp for an instant, then suddenly slackening. It was wonderfully refreshing.

'It's not hot,' I shouted to Matthias as he prepared to enter.

'You say it's hot?'

'It's *not* hot.'

'Right.' He joined us with a splash, wasting no time in testing the water. 'I see what you mean,' he said, gasping, 'most invigorating.'

'Matthias, do you always enter water in that fashion?' Jens asked, wading alongside.

'Not in the future.'

'We'd better swim somewhere before we die,' I said, beginning to feel cold again.

'Let's go to the other side then.' We all swam breaststroke, unhurriedly heading to the opposite bank. For the next half an hour we swam and rested and messed about without thoughts of anything but the present. Above us the sky was deep and clear like a fabulous jewel, as if we were all a part of an exotic gift to be worn on the finger of some transcendent deity. After a while I began to tire, my arms growing weak, and it was time to leave the water.

'Did you enjoy yourself?' Matthias's girlfriend asked as I took the towel from my bag.

'Yes, it wasn't too cold when we kept moving.' I felt embarrassed at not knowing her name. I couldn't even remember whether I had ever been told.

'Would you like some sun lotion?' she asked.

'Oh hell, yes, I forgot about that.' In the coolness of the lake I had given no thought to sun-cream. It seemed a stupid thing to forget, leaving me to wonder whether I was already condemned to burn the next day. I dried myself and applied the lotion, hoping that it was not too late, before settling down to idly watch Jens and Matthias splashing around.

'How long are you staying in Germany for?' the girl asked.

'Another week. I've been here a week already.'

'How do you know Jens?'

'We were at university together, in England.' My body felt completely refreshed, cleansed by the water and the sun. 'So, what do you do?'

'I'm still at university, studying politics. I graduate next year.'

'What are you going to do then?'

'I don't know. Perhaps more study.'

'That's the way, stay a student for as long as you can.'

Jens and Matthias climbed back up the bank, jokingly debating some point.

'It's good to have been cold, then warm, and now hot,' Matthias said, sitting on a wide tree root.

'Absolutely.' Jens dropped down next to me. 'Should we buy a drink?' he asked, rubbing himself with his towel.

The tall glasses that people were drinking from around us looked as enticing as the lake had earlier been, the glass shimmering against the blues and greens of the hazy afternoon. In the end though we decided not to buy alcohol, somehow it did not quite seem fitting, and so spent the next hour just relaxing on the rough lakeside. I was completely at peace, all troubles far away, floating in spirit among the whispers of the glittering air. Eventually Matthias and his girlfriend announced that they had to leave, saying that they were going on to meet a friend in a different town, so after saying goodbye and 'see you again,' Jens and I decided to change and then make our way home.

The journey back was much easier than the trip out had been. I managed to cycle with reasonable proficiency, enjoying the experience and the tranquillity of the aging day. For once the sun was pleasant, invigorating instead of mind dulling.

We arrived at Jens's house in a little over half an hour and were greeted by his mother.

'My mother asks how you found the cycle,' Jens told me.

'Good, though I was rather slow.' We all walked out into the back garden, to a table beneath a tree.

'We're going to eat here,' Jens continued. 'Shall we bring the things out?'

I went back into the kitchen with him and we brought out plates and food, setting them carefully on the table; it was pleasant to feel that I was making myself useful in some small way. Jens's father arrived with many a smile concerning my cycling, and the meal began. We ate slices of bread and cheese, cut meat and sausage. I was hungry and the food was lovely, the conversation similar to that of the earlier meal as I managed to communicate in a basic manner with the parents, though I wished more than ever that I could speak German. When we were finished, Jens and his mother cleared the table and I sat with the father.

'What time should we leave?' Jens asked, glancing back over his shoulder.

'Would about an hour be okay?'

'That's fine.'

Making use of hand gestures and eye contact I felt that Jens's father and I communicated rather well, one of us making the occasional comment and then trying to explain it to the other. Sometimes we spent five minutes on the same point, and sometimes we understood each other almost straight away. We drank a couple of bottles of beer together, the slightly bitter taste drifting through the mind into the warmth of early evening.

After a while Jens returned and we decided that we should be heading back into the city. I said goodbye to his parents and they waited by the front door as we drove away.

'So, have you enjoyed your day?' Jens asked.

'Yes, it's been great.'

'When you are next in Germany you should stay again.'

'Definitely.' I began to muse about when my next visit to the Continent would be. Watching Jens smoothly change gear I wondered how ordered his life was, whether he was happy or not. I was glad to be going back to Eva, but a part of me was yearning for another day of peace.

It took us a while to find the right road because Jens was not familiar with the area of the city. Eventually we arrived and I climbed out onto the pavement.

'Thanks for the lift, and for everything.'

'My pleasure. We must meet again before you leave.'

'Yes, I'll phone you sometime. Give my regards to your parents.'

'Goodnight.' He drove off, and I stood for a moment looking at the road before entering the flat.

'Did you have a good time?' Eva asked, opening the door of her apartment.

'Yes, but it's nice to be back again.' It really was nice. In fact, I felt rather ashamed for having half-wished that I could spend another day with Jens.

'Did you miss me?'

'Of course.' I was thrilled that she had asked.

Eva was in a happy mood that evening, but she was also tired and it wasn't long before she went to bed. Laying on the sofa once again, comparing my position to that of the previous night, I reflected on what an unusually cheerful day it had been. Nothing in particular had been accomplished, but I had enjoyed a time-out from the emotional struggles that were such a constant drain. Most importantly of all, I had been a part of family life. This was something that Eva's exciting yet cold flat lacked. It occurred to me that I had never before really understood the importance of family.

Chapter Seven

It was not a happy few minutes that I spent waiting for Eva outside the university office where she was engaged in a discussion with her tutor. The Wednesday afternoon seemed to have lasted forever, yet time was slipping away as surely as the summer day melting to evening. I perched on a table in the deserted corridor, sliding one foot over the grey, stone floor, noting its patterns sculpted by random marks; from far away there echoed shouts and slamming doors as the academic clock wound itself down once more.

Since my stay with Jens, Eva and I had drawn closer in some ways, but there was still no contentment or satisfaction. I had wanted to return from Germany with a new hope, with the ability to enjoy life at home whilst looking forward to our next meeting, without the stifling anxiety. Now it seemed that this would not be the case, as thoughts of the slow death of distant love, of men in nightclubs and university dining halls attacked my mind. The very posters on the walls, so familiar yet so distant, were enough to stir my heart—I wondered whether I would ever see the same corridor, live the same scalding life, again. Each of the last three days had been mostly spent in the university, and it was strange to consider how much time I had spent waiting in the library or in a computer room while Eva attended her classes.

Eva stalked out of the office, the look in her eye suggesting that nothing particularly good or bad had come from the meeting, yet there was something almost aggressive in her movements.

'Okay?' I queried.

'Yes, we're all happy with the way that things are going.' She led the way down the corridor. 'Are we going to eat at home?'

'I don't mind.' On consideration it occurred to me that a meal out would be more romantic, would let people see us together. 'Actually, why don't we eat at a restaurant somewhere?'

'It'll have to be somewhere cheap.'

'I'll pay for it.'

'Thanks, but it'll still have to be somewhere cheap.'

'I suppose so.' She was right, of course. My supply of German currency was running low, and although I could withdraw more if required, it was important not to let expenses run out of control. If we were in England, I thought, then it would be possible for me to plan things properly, to find a good restaurant that offered reasonable prices and book a table in advance. This, of course, was not a possibility in our current situation.

Leaving the university, we walked through the main street of the town. The early evening was a mixture of the remains of daytime life—shoppers and businessmen—and the stirrings of the approaching night, made up of the first party seekers on their way to make an early start at the festival. The scene was a mass of understated colour, issuing from the crowds, the cold buildings, the dome of sky, even the old paving beneath us—veteran of years of changing footfall. We stopped at a tiny Italian restaurant. It was really nothing more than a kitchen with a few plastic tables both inside and outside the shop, serving hatches giving access to both areas. A menu was chalked out on a blackboard fixed below the hatch.

'We could eat here if you want,' Eva suggested. 'It might be nice to sit outside.'

'If you don't mind all these people walking past.' The white tables were in an alcove, set back from the still busy street. I gave Eva the money and she went to the serving hatch, ordering us both spaghetti bolognaise which was on special offer.

'It'll take ten minutes to be ready,' she said, sitting next to me. A man with a huge dog on a chain walked past, his eyes fixed meaninglessly on some unknown point in front of him.

'My mother says that I should find a job for the summer,' Eva continued. 'Apparently there are vacancies at the fast-food place here. Do you think that I should apply for a job?'

'Do you want to?'

'I don't know. The money would be nice.'

'Well, it's up to you.' I paused for a moment. This seemed as good a time as any to breach the subject of our next meeting. 'Just, I was hoping—'

'What?'

'A part of me was hoping that you'd be free over the summer, so that we could do something together.'

'I wouldn't be working all the time. You could come and stay with me again. It would just be a part-time job to make some money.'

'Eva, when are we going to meet each other again?' She was silent, embarrassed. 'Talk to me, darling, I need some input.'

'The trouble is, it would be very difficult for me to visit you in England, with my mother being so ill.'

'You couldn't leave her for a couple of weeks, even?'

'I could, but if anything happened while I was away then I'd feel like it was my fault.'

'Yes, I understand.' I vaguely noticed a group of children laugh their way past us. 'So, what are we going to do?'

'When will you be able to visit here again?'

'I don't know. I can really only afford to make one more trip this summer, so we'd better leave it till later on, because after that I guess we won't be able to meet again until Christmas.' Summer, Christmas, Easter—the cost and the problems of sorting out when and where to meet, stretching away into the unknown, no finishing point in sight, having always to balance responsibilities. I wished that we could put everyone else aside, be utterly irresponsible for a while, think only of ourselves for a day or two. 'Well, we'll sort something out any-way. It'll be fine.'

I wanted to be with Eva, I didn't want to go home because I wanted to be with her all the time. Yet if we were ever going to be together permanently then many issues would have to be solved. For one thing, living with each other was more difficult than I had imagined it would be. Somehow it was impossible to avoid getting on each other's nerves a lit-tle when always in such close proximity to one another. I could see how domestic rows over silly things like washing up could start—a boiling tension you feel towards the other person sud-denly spilling over. However, if we were able to live a little more comfortably and free from worry then I felt that this would not be the case with us.

The meal arrived shortly, long strands of spaghetti sur-rounding the beef sauce. The spaghetti was embarrassing to eat because I couldn't work out how to wind it successfully around the fork. Either it would collapse as soon as it approached my mouth or else there was always one strand that hung loose and that had to be sucked up in a most undig-nified manner.

'You should try cutting it smaller,' Eva suggested.

'I know, but it's still hard to pick up.' I felt like a barbar-ian attempting a romantic meal. It was made worse by the fact that Eva seemed to have no difficulty with her food, and although she said nothing more there was a slight look of dis-gust in her face, as if she could not quite believe that anybody could find eating a meal so complicated. I struggled for twenty minutes, splashing sauce, inwardly cursing the sneaky strands with their powerful survival instinct, until eventually regard-ing the still sizable remnants of my meal, I decided that enough was enough.

'I think I'll leave the rest of this. It was very nice though.'

'What shall we do tonight?' Eva asked. 'Would you like to return to the festival?'

'Actually, I'm quite tired today.' I felt that I could not face the festival atmosphere any longer. I was ragged inside, worn down by paranoid jealousies. 'Why don't we go for a walk somewhere instead?'

'If you want.' She considered for a moment. 'I could take you to another of our parks, where there are some remains of old buildings.'

'Ah, historical stuff.'

'Yes. There used to be a huge, open-air theatre, and parts of it are still there. It's quite interesting.'

'Let's go there then,' I said, glad that we had avoided all kinds of nightclub.

We caught the bus home so that Eva could leave her university bag behind, and then took another bus to the park. The journey took half an hour, though with many stops it was difficult to tell how far we were from home, the streets all very similar despite altering styles of building and the occasional parade of shops.

'This is the first time I've been here for over a year,' Eva told me as we left the bus. The park lay before us, a huge expanse of wilting grass with wide paths cut across it. It was busier than I had expected, cyclists and skateboarders shooting across the concrete areas between dog walkers and solitary ramblers.

'Where's the old theatre?' I asked.

'We have to follow the path for a bit; you can't see it at the moment.'

It was a pleasant stroll, through the shouts of children and chatter of birds, though I was so weary with the efforts of the past days that even walking was uncomfortably tiring. I felt like we were an army in retreat. At least the feared sunburn had never materialised; on Sunday morning I had woken half expecting the skin around my shoulders to be raw and itching, but nothing had come of it.

'It's lucky that my mother doesn't go out much anymore,' Eva said, 'or else she might be here. This was a favourite place at one time, she used to bring me here when I was a small child.'

Eva's concern about us accidentally meeting her mother had passed onto me to some extent. Not so much when we were out, but I would have felt very embarrassed had her mother unexpectedly arrived at the flat. The previous day there had been a knock at the door and we had both jumped, my heart beating fast as Eva went to answer it. In the end it had only been a neighbour, but all the same I sat in the living room with the door closed until the neighbour had gone, and it all seemed very wrong.

As always, the reminder that I was living as a fugitive caused a flush of frustration to pass though my body. Why couldn't she tell her mother about me? Was it really just about age? And she and her mother had come here when she was very young. I realised that this would have been before I was born, long before. It was almost painful to think that she had lived much of her childhood before I was alive, that each stage of her development into an adult had been before mine, as if this made her past into a greater, sadder, mystery. While I was being wheeled in my pram she was almost a teenager, as I began secondary school she had already reached her twenties. And as we sauntered through the green evening I thought more deeply about age, about why it was that I found Eva's age so attractive and what implications this held for the future. If we were still together in ten years then would her beauty have faded with approaching middle age, and would I in my late twenties still find her attractive in her late thirties?

Thinking of the past, I tried to imagine what the city and the park would have been like one hundred years before. Would there have been mothers with their young children here then—children who would be dead by now, anyway? I could almost imagine us walking here through the Victorian gardens, so much history still unwritten. But then—how could any of this have existed before Eva was born?

> Gray goose and gander,
> Waft your wings together,
> And carry the good king's daughter
> Over the one strand river.

Rounding a bend in the path we arrived at the sight of the old theatre, previously hidden from view. The layers of stone seating were still intact, cracked and grey, and beneath them a paved area which must have been the stage. It was a huge construction.

'When was it built?' I asked.

'I'm not sure; actually I've never really wondered. The kids love it here.'

'They certainly do.' Skateboarders, mainly between about eight and fourteen years old, covered all parts of the structure, displaying varying levels of skill and sometimes coming close to collapsing down the steps in what could be a horrible accident.

'It's a wonder nobody gets killed,' I said, sensing that Eva was having similar thoughts.

Walking along the edge of the ruined theatre, avoiding bicycles and skateboards, was an unsettling experience. I could not tell exactly why, but that the great void opened once again between me and Eva, so strong that it felt as though one of us did not exist in the present. The strange thought occurred to me that she was a traveller in time, that the universe was mixed up so that she belonged to the age in which the theatre was built, but had been somehow superimposed on my consciousness. It seemed for a moment that the two ages were fused together, that we walked through both the present day and whatever dreaming past the cold stones around us had been erected for. There was certainly something sinister about the place; the memory of countless generations of hope, pain, and eventual futility reeked from the drabness of the ruins. Indeed, the past was very close to us then, haunting our movements, just out of sight.

'Let's go away from here a bit,' Eva suggested. 'I don't want to be run over by a skateboard.'

'Good idea.' I wondered whether she was feeling the coldness of the area as well. As we continued down the path she took hold of my hand, and this drew us together again, the warmth of her fingers like the light of morning that banishes the nightmare. Maybe, I thought, everything will turn out all right. Maybe we could find a way around our problems, learn to live with them.

'If we keep going in this direction then eventually we'll arrive back where we started,' Eva said, glancing back down the path for a moment.

'That's good then, we'll get a circular walk.'

We completed the circuit of the park and arrived back at the bus stop. Glancing at my watch I was surprised by how late it was, nearly ten o'clock and the sky beginning to dull. Eva checked the timetable.

'It'll be twenty minutes before the bus arrives,' she told me, and the fact that we would have to wait caused me to feel a sense of nervous irritation. There was a certain uncomfortable feel to the area, the deserted city street in the fading day. It seemed as though violence was close at hand beneath the emotional destitution of the bleak rows of houses, with each approaching figure causing me an uncanny fear as it neared us. I longed to be back at the flat, safely hidden from the dangerous possibilities of the night.

When the bus arrived I felt so relieved that I was a little embarrassed by my earlier concern. We made the trip home; arriving back at the apartment before darkness fell, glad to arrive at the end of a tiring day.

'Tomorrow we should book the train tickets for your return journey,' Eva told me as we sat at the kitchen table. 'I won't be able to come to Frankfurt with you, because of university. It's a shame you're not going home on Saturday, then I could have accompanied you.'

'Well, I had to book for Friday to get the best deal.' I was dreading Friday's journey to Frankfurt. Having to go across the country on my own was a challenge that I would rather not have faced.

'Before university tomorrow we can go to the local station and buy your tickets,' she continued. 'It's best to do it a day in advance, just in case there's a problem.'

'Absolutely. And then, I guess, I'm off on my own.' I could hardly believe that in just two days we would be apart again. 'I'll start arrangements for my next visit as soon as I get home.'

'And maybe when we next meet I'll have a job,' she smiled. 'We'll have to go on a nice trip sometime.'

'Yes, perhaps we could take a short holiday somewhere at Christmas.'

'I'll have to see how my mother is, but maybe we could.'

We continued to talk vaguely about the future, but I knew that, until I arrived back in England, my imminent departure would be uppermost in both our minds.

And so, at nine o'clock the following morning, we climbed the few steps that led to the train station by the university and entered through the automatic doors. It was a nerve-wracking building for me, a symbol of the next day's frightening journey. Eva led the way into a large room with a number of desks behind which sat officials giving information and handing out tickets, looking like cashiers at a bank. There was a small queue, and while we waited I glanced around the walls, noticing the maps of various routes and connections, in colours of blue, green and red. It was all so serious; there was even a serious odour to the room, something to do with stone floors and whirring computers. Despite the heat of the day outside there was a certain feeling of dampness to the place, perhaps caused by the constant passage of individuals, stopping here to plan a journey before vanishing back into their distant lives.

'There's no direct connection,' Eva said on reaching the front of the queue and conversing with the official, 'so you'll have to change a couple of times.'

'Okay.' This was disastrous. I had been counting on there being a direct line to Frankfurt, which would mean that so long as I left the train at the correct stop, nothing could go wrong. When the money was exchanged for tickets and we withdrew to the side of the room to study the printed connection sheet, I began to wonder whether I would ever make it home.

'The first part of the journey is quite short,' Eva was saying. 'You travel for about a quarter of an hour to this little town, and then take the train for Würzburg. Once there you change again for the train that goes through Frankfurt.'

'I hope it'll be clear when to change.' At home it would have been easy to make this relatively simple trip, but in a situation where one wrong move would leave me stranded, alone in a foreign country, and especially when I had no means of communicating with those around me, the potential for crisis seemed enormous.

'It won't be a problem; you just have to look for the signs. There'll probably be an electronic sign in the carriage telling you which station is coming up.'

'Yes, of course, it'll be fine.' It would, I told myself, be fine. But I wasn't quite convinced.

We left the station and began the unhurried walk to the university. The wide grass area by the main building was already stirring to the effects of the blistering heat; students ambled in light clothing, satchels hung loosely from one shoulder, the morning preparing to swallow up the remnants of early freshness. I knew that I would dream of such scenes when back at home, however painful they were I would still dream of them and miss them.

Chapter Eight

That Thursday evening, being my last before departure, we went for a stroll along the riverside, starting out on the same route that we had followed the previous Saturday. The heat of the day had slackened, creating a certain sense of calm, yet my nerves were in a state of high confusion; a mixture of worry about the coming journey, frustration over my situation with Eva, and concern for the future.

We ambled down the grey road, past groups of children playing in the water and cyclists swerving along their designated lane. I was desperate to do something to show Eva that I loved her, but my mind froze every time I tried to focus on the issue.

'So, my train leaves at one o'clock tomorrow afternoon,' I said at length. 'Strange to think that I'll be gone in eighteen hours.'

'Yes.' Her reply seemed so stale, so wearisome that it was difficult to know how to continue the conversation.

'But we'll meet again soon,' I tried.

'Of course.'

There was not, I thought, anything particularly upsetting about the way in which she was behaving. It was merely that a certain show of emotion would have made everything so much more hopeful. Again, it saddened me to think how beautiful she looked, how at home she was in her city. Sometimes it felt as though we were only playing at being a couple, that neither of us would ever be able to leave our individual homes and lives in order to commit to each other.

'Shall we go on the bridge?' Eva suggested. We had reached the old, brooding bridge that had disturbed me at the weekend. For some reason it did not look so awful the second time, perhaps because it was deserted.

Reaching the top of the dark steps, we walked to the point overlooking the middle of the river, and stood for a moment in silence. The water passed silently beneath us, barely alive for all its icy mass. Suddenly we were far from the rest of the evening, the two of us alone with all movement belonging to a different world. It was unsettling, somehow hopeless — tomorrow we part again.

'Look at the sky,' Eva said, pointing heavenwards. 'There's just a single cloud.'

I peered upwards. Indeed, a solitary cloud floated above us in the ageless blue, almost mockingly; I could hardly believe that it was the same sky under which my own home rested. It seemed at first to have the shape of a face, then changed into a whirlpool as it slid onwards towards the horizon. They call it cloud gazing, I thought, when you watch the clouds and try to analyse your subconscious by the shapes you see in them. What patterns, what unknowns are hidden at the corners of the mind? For an instant I considered asking Eva what she saw, but somehow I knew that she would not understand.

We crossed the bridge and walked back along the river, on the other side. The day continued to weaken, into that summer bracket between early evening and night when most of the long rush dissolves to tranquillity. The riverside grass was swarming with laughing children, like memories of all childhoods. We turned away from the water, into a part of the city that was entirely new to me. It was older than Eva's quarter, the dusty steps and flower border stone belonging to past generations. Still, I wanted so much to bring Eva closer to me, to do something that would seal our love, make it official, bring me hope when we had to part. Yet as we passed over the stone squares beside short houses my thoughts turned to missed opportunities, and I began to wonder whether my chance had already faded.

You could have told her you loved her; you could have taken the dominant role. She's just shy about love, she always needs you to make the first move. You haven't even kissed her properly yet. But it doesn't matter because I know we're in love. It's natural to take the physical side slowly in such a relationship. But how about when you leave? Think of all those other men. You've been here two weeks now, there have been so many moments when you could have achieved something; you have to act NOW.

'Shall we stop somewhere for some food or drink?' I suggested. It occurred to me that, were we able to sit down, we might be able to talk about the future.

'If you want,' Eva spoke without enthusiasm. 'Do you want to?'

'I don't mind,' I lied. We approached an Italian restaurant, a red-brick building with a battered sign set up on the street before a small garden of flowers; serene beyond the pattering footfall of the pathways. 'Shall we stop here?'

'Do you really want to?'

'I thought you might,' I said, trying to hide my exasperation.

'We could eat at home. It'd be cheaper.'

'If you want to,' I gave up.

We continued down narrow streets, the grey memorials of bygone times shaped in walls and cracked window panes; eventually turning out onto a large field. Stalls were set out along a main path, selling drinks, ice creams and trinkets. There were quite a few people around, and it had the feel of a small carnival near the end of the day. Neither of us was particularly interested in the stalls, but we browsed around for a while before continuing through the park and onto a path that rejoined the river.

The water was much wider at this point, laying to our right and making the opposite bank seem quite distant. To our left there was more parkland, populated by a few couples with dogs. I gazed across the silent grass, up to where the city buildings rose in the middle distance, and my heart stirred with sadness. This, I thought, was far, far away from my life. The scene was familiar but I did not belong, soon it would all be a dream. And as we walked it seemed that nothing existed but ourselves, as though a bubble surrounded us through which nothing, no thought or vision, could pass. Hardly speaking, we reached a point where the parkland to the left gave way to houses; large, ugly modern blocks of defeat. It was still warm, but a chill had fallen on my soul, and suddenly everything was desolate. We passed an old playground, little remaining but a hard, concrete surface where a few bored teenagers loitered. The few people who we saw were not smiling or talking, but dragging their way onwards in a stupor. Beyond the grey, bleakness of the barren water, tower blocks thrust upwards, their empty windows as lifeless as the roadside stones. One tower caught my eye in particular, a tall gleaming structure, reflecting the evening sun. It was surreal, like something from science fiction, windows seeming to hide inexplicable glimpses of mystery.

'What building is that?' I asked, pointing.

'It's new,' Eva replied. 'It was built when I was in England. I think it's the headquarters of some company.'

We paused for a while, and in my mind I saw a story. The tower was an alien structure that had appeared one day and enslaved the inhabitants of the city, turning them into the emotionless beings that I saw around us. The region of the city beyond the river was an alien land that could never be reached, never understood by those who were contaminated by it. We were the last freedom fighters, facing almost certain failure but not quite giving up, desperate to smuggle somebody out of the city to alert the outside world. How far down did that black water go, I wondered? It seemed that the whole view in front of us was devoid of real life. Eva will remain here, I thought. She will remain a part of the city when I am gone. She can walk these streets again, see the same views whenever she wants, but I will not be with her.

'Let's head back now,' Eva suggested, breaking me out of my thoughts. I was more than happy to agree; we had been walking for a long time and there didn't seem to be any point in continuing.

It took half an hour to reach home, and in that time matters improved a little. We followed a wide pedestrian path that cut though the residential area, at one point passing though a square of shops and restaurants. Two middle-aged American men asked us for directions to a café.

'It's just there,' Eva said, pointing to a nearby building.

We joked with them for a few moments, and the lift that the humour gave to my soul made our surroundings a little less drab, as though some colour were returning. When they took their leave Eva seemed happier as well, more relaxed, and we held hands during the remainder of the walk home which, once again, caused the nightmare to recede, giving some warmth and pleasure to the evening.

An hour later, as we sat on the sofa with the television on, the frustration was bubbling within me again. I could almost see time slipping away in physical moments as the characters on the screen spoke in the unknown tongue, leaving me with nothing to do but brood while Eva became involved in the plot. Her physical presence was strong beside me, mixing desire with a sense of great failure.

'I think I'll go to bed soon,' she said eventually. 'We have to get up early tomorrow.'

'And I still have to pack my suitcase.' The smell of the flat was heavy in the air.

'Yes.' She switched off the television and stood up. I stood as well and put my arms around her, pulling her towards me.

'I love you, Eva.'

'I'm not in the mood.' She broke away, but I pulled her back again.

'I don't know, darling,' I said. 'It's all so complicated.' She was silent. I tried to think how to continue, but it wasn't much good, everything was suddenly impulsive. 'I know it's not easy, but I do love you.' We were both silent for a moment, but

I could see that she was moved. 'I just wondered whether you had the same feelings for me.'

'Yes.' She spoke as though she was afraid of the word, as though by agreeing that we were in love she was betraying herself, but it was a relief to hear all the same.

'Well, that's nice to know.'

'We should get on.' She pulled away from me and began arranging her books for the next day. I set about the task of packing my suitcase, a strange job, as I could not quite believe that I was about to go home. Everything was quite surreal; we had finally held the big conversation but time was moving on all the same.

Later that evening, when Eva had gone to bed, I stood at the window for a long time, thinking about the past couple of weeks and trying to imagine the future. Looking around the living room I realised that, although I had grown used to the flat, it did not feel like a home. It was more a place of under-stated drama, washed by interlacing despair and sudden hope. Yet the row of mugs on the dresser, the black wooden table upon which a pile of dusty magazines rested, the old red curtains; all had become a part of me, a part of my struggle.

I thought of the ways in which Eva seemed to have changed since I had known her at university. Then it had been me who had looked after her, but now the roles were more often reversed. It was as though she had become less innocent, more sure of herself, but not always in a pleasant way. Was this the same girl with whom I had strolled through those soft spring lanes? Yes, of course nothing had changed much, just we knew each other more deeply now; reality was replacing that first enthralling enchantment with a different kind of magic. Yet I longed for us to be back in England together, where I did not feel so out of place, among the daffodil yellow of our earliest romance.

And it was strange and lonely, standing at the window with Eva asleep in the next room, so close yet out of reach. We had said that we loved each other, but there were still so many other things that we needed to discuss that it didn't change anything much. Outside, the city was warm and quiet in the few back gardens and shadowy walls that fell in view. I let my mind wander over its multitude of streets, from the ancient centre of medieval walls to the modern dusty white flats. This, I knew, was a place that I would forever walk in dreams. That alien tower would return to me at night—for what sits at the top of the tower?

The black outline of a cat scuttled across the garden, barely visible. There was so much out there; violence and peace turning within the thousands of common lives that could never quite be ordinary. I could feel the city turning around us in all its mystery—a living, eternal being that defies understanding. Yet for all its secrets I could imagine glimpses of everyday events occurring. On a road a mile away, perhaps, a drunk teenager was throwing an empty beer can into a garden; in a two-room apartment an old man fell asleep reading a book; somewhere close by a couple argued over money—all their lives a tiny part of the whole.

So much history was evident that it seemed more real than the present. The city centre, which had once housed the great minds of the Renaissance, emanated its spirit outwards to the suburbs. It would take an hour to walk to the centre, and yet it was linked to Eva's flat by streets of buildings and homes. Somehow the flat was connected to history. Eva lived every day in the shadow of the past, walking along the abandoned Victorian railway track or past decaying houses of the nineteen-twenties. It was frightening and rather sad to think how lost in time everything seemed to be. I was glad to be inside; the night without seemed haunted by half-understood fears. Yet, as I gazed across space to the opposite block of flats, noting the lights in certain windows, I still could not believe that the next day I would be gone.

At ten o'clock the following morning I sat in the computer lab of the university, staring with little interest at the shimmering screen. My mind was replaying the unreal events of the morning—leaving the flat with my awkward suitcase, waiting for a bus in the headache of the dusty street, sensing the slightly

exotic impression of the waking city. Eva and I had spoken little on the bus, largely because it was so hard to think of anything worth saying. It was as though all that could be achieved
had been achieved for the time being. Yet as we strolled
through the university grounds I had felt again the heavy sen-
sual nature of her body, something in the way she walked and
held herself, of the sun and the shape of her legs beneath her
skirt, and again it was almost tragic.

The computer lab was quite busy but the atmosphere was
friendly. At first when I had spent time alone in the library or
on the computers I had worried that somebody would speak to
me in German, causing embarrassment, but it didn't seem to
matter anymore. Today, Eva was busy with a seminar until
eleven o'clock, and then we had arranged to meet Jens for
lunch before heading to the station for my one o'clock departure.

Using the Internet, I looked up various cricket sites, reading the results for the season so far. It was oddly exciting to be
going home again, exciting as well as heart-rending and illu-
sory.

For the field is full of shades as I near the shadowy coast,
And a ghostly batsman plays to the bowling of a ghost.

The sound of tapping keys echoed from all around, with an
occasional mutter from one friend to another. I thought about
the journey to Frankfurt, what trains would have to be caught
and what difficulties lay ahead. If I could make it to Frankfurt
station without any disasters then I guessed that the rest of the
trip home would not be a problem.

Reading a page dedicated to the development of cricket
in third world countries, I looked up and saw an older man
peer into the room for a moment, as if he were searching for
someone, and then withdraw again. He wore glasses and his
hair was greying, face lined but handsome. I wondered
whether he was a student or a teacher—he had the look of a
professor.

The room continued to click around me as time wore down, until Eva returned just after eleven and we walked to the canteen to meet Jens at half past the hour.

'I remember we came here on my first Tuesday,' I said, feeling that the meeting would be rather a sad rerun of earlier days. 'That was when we arranged for me to spend the Sunday with Jens.'

'That's right.' Eva led the way up the stairs. It was very busy in the canteen with a great rush at the counter. Jens was already waiting for us and we queued together, watching the bustle of the diners in their sports shirts and jeans. I chose a pie meal, but didn't feel much like eating, my stomach full from nerves.

'When do you plan to return next?' Jens asked, cutting into his fish.

'I'm not sure. Perhaps August or September.'

'Will Eva visit you in England?' We both glanced at her.

'I can't really. I have to work.'

'What job are you going to get?' Jens enquired.

'Maybe at the fast-food place.'

'You should get a better job,' I said, with some feeling. 'They work you pretty hard in those places for not much money.'

'My mother thinks that I should do something.'

'Well, think about it carefully,' I replied, resisting the temptation to point out that she was old enough to make her own decisions.

Every few minutes I glanced at my watch, regretting the fact that it was impossible to relax with the journey imminent.

'Matthias apologises for being unable to join us,' Jens said, at length.

'That's okay, I'm sure he's got a lot of things to do.'

'He says that he enjoyed our day out on Sunday though.'

'That was fun. Perhaps next time I come we can go out again.'

'Yes, but the lake will not be so warm later on.' Jens laughed, taking a big gulp of his fruit drink.

'What are you doing for the rest of the day?' I asked.

'I have just one hour of lecture, from three until four.'

'That's not too bad.' I felt a little envious of Jens; his home was only a bus ride away.

We finished our meal, and by then it was well after midday and time to leave. The nerves rose higher within me; I knew that once I was on the train it would be easier, the worst trials are those that have not yet begun, but as we walked back out into the street I could barely comprehend the coming hours.

'So, what can I say?' Jens faced me outside the building.

'Well, we shall probably meet again in a few months.'

'Yes, I hope so. Have a good journey and take care.'

'Thank you. Say hello to your parents for me.'

'I will. Goodbye, Dave, goodbye, Eva.' He turned and walked away down the busy street. We didn't stop to watch him go, but headed straight for the station as time was running short. Emotionally, I barely noticed him leave. Saying goodbye to a friend was easy, I thought, friendship is so much easier than love.

My suitcase banged against my leg as we hurried down the road to the station. Descending the black, uninviting stairs we trotted though the subterranean passage, passing a newspaper stand and dozens of lost, worn-looking people, before climbing up to our platform with fifteen minutes to spare. I was surprised to find how empty the platform was; just ourselves and an elderly couple on the bare, isolated strip of land. We sat on one of the long benches, the sky pouring its heat against the few trees and the dying grass. Eva looked radiantly attractive, this becoming horribly frustrating, almost derisive.

'This doesn't seem real,' I said, meaning it.

'No.' Eva replied without enthusiasm. I wondered what she was thinking about.

'Eight minutes to go then.' My mind was on the journey ahead, and this stopped me from feeling as sad as I might have done. The lowest moments, I knew, would come later; it would take a while to come to terms with the situation.

'I'm going to make enquires about my next visit as soon as I get home,' I said, 'look up travel costs and things.'

'Do that.'

'You know,' I said wistfully, 'it would be really nice if you could come and stay with me in England at some point.'

'As I say, it's difficult. You know that I'd like to.'

'Yes, darling, I know that.'

'And I have to think about my mother.'

'Yes, of course. But, Eva?'

'Yes?'

'I do love you.'

'Yes, don't worry. It'll be all right.'

It seemed to take a long time for the train to arrive. Eva was distant and distracted, probably thinking about her afternoon university work. She let me hold her hand, though I had the impression that she would have preferred not to. Somehow, it didn't matter. I was beginning to think that the small physical things were not always so important.

A little of the afternoon drifted past, and the train arrived on time. I heard it rattling towards us long before it came into view, like a huge, mechanical serpent.

'This is it then,' I stood and picked up the suitcase.

'So, I wish you a pleasant journey,' Eva said, sounding cold and formal, though I guessed without intending to.

'We'll see each other again before long.' This was impossible, but it was happening nonetheless. The train slowed to a standstill and the doors hissed open.

'Well, goodbye.'

'Goodbye, darling.' I squeezed her hand for a moment before climbing into the carriage. Almost immediately the train began to move and the platform was sliding away. Eva waved and then turned back towards the station. It was an unsatisfying goodbye, but my departure had not yet sunk in, and my mind was so confused as to be numb.

There was nobody else in the small carriage. Alone with the sweet, interior odour I flopped down on a seat and examined my ticket. So, that was it. Eva was left behind. Eva was left behind and in fifteen minutes I had to make a connection. There were green fields with the grey buildings behind them, but Eva was gone and there was a connection to be made. I wondered how fast we were travelling, how far away Eva was with every passing minute, imagining how long it would take me to walk back to her.

The city faded from the window, and before long we arrived at the next station. The change was easy, down onto the hot platform and a short walk to where the next train was already waiting. There were only three platforms; a small outpost of the metropolis left behind. Two minutes of standstill and we moved off again.

It was a relief to have made the first connection; now there was the long trip to Würzburg with nothing to do but sit and watch the scenery, yet I felt the passing seconds distancing me from Eva with a strange, detached pain. My new carriage contained two old men and a woman with a young, sleeping child. The floor of the central aisle was dirty with muddy footprints and there was an empty drink bottle lying on one seat, but otherwise it was a comfortable, rattling trip.

I settled into my seat, thinking only about Eva and the rest of the journey. It was almost romantic, beginning what would be a twenty-two hour passage across Europe and back home. In my mind I could see a map with a red trail marking my progress. It would be less romantic at Frankfurt station though, I guessed. I expected to arrive there at around six o'clock, and my coach was not leaving until ten. Why, though, was Eva so detached at times, so distant? Why had I not made more use of the time that I had? She seemed insistent on seeing our relationship as directly opposed to her usual life, especially to her mother, as if by spending time with me she was making a betrayal. What would it be like to meet her mother? I wished that I could meet her. I wished that everybody in the world knew about our relationship; as matters stood, all of Eva's family would think that she was single. This hurt, and cut me with jealousy. Yes, I thought, most people must think that she's single. And look at the way she dresses, those skirts with the slits right the way up, some men must think that she's up for the taking. No, she's sensible enough not to get into any trouble. Somehow, though, even the thoughts of other men were enough to agonize me.

An hour passed and there were mountains once again, the same that we had seen on the outbound trip almost two weeks before. They still reeked of mystery, colours of purple and brown, gleaming through the high haze of the afternoon. There was a strong companionship between a couple, I thought. Somehow you become bound to one another, as if you have always known each other. It becomes a family thing. I could not imagine ever being as close to anybody as I was to Eva. We were family; in fact it felt as though we were married. It did not seem possible that we could ever sever that link.

An inspector smiled his way down the aisle. He examined my ticket for a moment, causing my heart to leap, but then stamped it and moved on. I knew that we were approaching Würzburg and that finding the right connection could be difficult; however, a forty-minute wait was scheduled, so I assumed that this would give me enough time.

We began to slow a long time before reaching the station. My heart rate increased as we arrived, passengers spilling out onto the waiting concrete. With suitcase beginning to grow tiresome, I consulted a wall map and walked to the platform from which I was set to depart. There were many businessmen around, black suits and ties, all with briefcases and mobile phones. They were like a bug that inhabits every civilised part of the world, harmless and barely noticeable after a while, even comforting.

There was a train already waiting at the platform, and although half an hour remained before I was due to leave, I wondered if it might be mine. A lot of people were already boarding and I thought that if I waited there might be no seats left. A guard was standing a short distance away, and I approached him.

'Excuse me, is this the train for Frankfurt?'

'*Wie, bitte?*'

I thought he might not have heard properly. 'Is this the Frankfurt train?'

He shook his head, clearly unable to speak English. I smiled and retreated, cursing my linguistic defects. Should I risk boarding the train or not?

I wished that Eva or Jens were with me, or just about any-body. These problems were not half as bad when there was a friend to share the consequences of any decision. I decided to wait until ten minutes before my departure time and then review the situation. A few lone travellers boarded the train, huge piles of luggage loaded with considerable difficulty, brown and black bulging containers. Fifteen minutes passed as the anxiety increased. Another guard appeared and I caught his eye.

'Excuse me, is this the train for Frankfurt?'

'Pardon?' He was a kind-looking man, of later middle age. I wondered what he would be like to know personally.

'Is this the train for Frankfurt?'

'Frankfurt? Yes.'

'Thanks.' It was a huge relief. Climbing up, I was able to find a seat in one of the busy carriages, sitting next to an eld-erly bald man who seemed content to stare at his newspaper without actually reading it. We moved off at the correct time, gathering speed and ending my brief visit to Würzburg.

The rest of the journey to Frankfurt was uneventful until we neared our destination and I began to worry that I would somehow miss the stop. Scenery floated past, the trees thirsty and the air crackling with the secrecy of its heat. The old man next to me left at an earlier station, and nobody took his place. It was sad though, the empty seat. When I closed my eyes, feel-ing the gentle rhythm of our passage, I felt sure that Eva was sitting beside me. I had grown so used to travelling with her on trains and buses that I could hardly believe it when I turned my head and there was nothing by my side but the vacant cushion.

Eventually we began to slow and, assuming that we were about to arrive, I left my carriage and waited by one of the exit doors. A woman with a suitcase was standing in front of me, but when the train stopped she made no move, saying some-thing to me in German and laughing. I laughed as well, pre-tending that I could understand her. Without a window on the door I could not tell whether we had arrived, but perhaps, I thought, the woman was not leaving at this stop at all. If we were at the station then it might soon be too late. There were anxious moments, but just as I had decided to ask her to move aside so I could open the door I was startled by a great rush of noise as another train crashed past. With grim amusement I realised that we had not yet arrived at the station—if I had stepped outside I would have been killed. I wondered exactly what the woman had said to me.

We began to move again, stopping after two minutes, upon which the doors opened and I alighted onto Frankfurt station with four hours remaining before my coach departed. The place was dense with people, a melee of luggage and bad-tempered rush. It was so busy that I had to navigate a passage between the various oncoming bodies as I made my way off the platform and through to the main part of the station. It was very sad to think that this was the place where Eva and I met at the start of my visit, and I tried not to remember it too closely.

More to pass time that anything else, I went in search of the coach departure point, but found it without much diffi-culty. The coaches were parked on a lonely stretch of road behind the station, and one of them was preparing to leave. It seemed so awful that I had to wait for over three hours, with my stomach aching where I had not eaten for so long and my head heavy with tiredness. After a while I went back inside and sat beneath a pillar, watching the people move around me. The hours drifted past very, very slowly, while I was shaken by detached sadness at leaving Eva, and a great longing to be home.

There were hundreds of thousands of men and women in the city, and I knew not one of them. Beyond the station there were cars and buses whining through the streets, hotels glow-ing into the night with pleasant smells rising from restaurants, bars already crowded and smoky. Yet Eva was far away in her own city, moving through the evening without me, continuing as before I had arrived.

Picking his way between the crowds, an old man approached me and began to speak in German.

'Sorry?' I said.

'I need help,' he repeated in English, 'I have my wallet taken and have no money for the train home. I go to the police but the police cannot help.'

What the hell, I thought, and gave him fifty pfennig. There were a lot of beggars around, some of them really ragged, dead eyes staring from the flesh. I remembered the pigeons at the London coach station.

What I really wanted was a bed, to be able to sleep in a proper bed, not to drowse awkwardly on a coach. Better than the beggars, though — they don't have anywhere to sleep. I was starving as well, my stomach weak as though it had given up all hope of food that day. Eventually I went into one of the little shops and bought some bread, bringing it back to the pillar to eat. It had a warm taste, like a memory of the place I had left behind. I wondered what Eva was doing, whether she was thinking about me, and when we would meet each other again.

Sitting between the tramps and the slowly thinning multitudes, beneath the high, white ceiling and smell of cleaning fluid, I waited for time to ease itself away. There was so much to think about that eventually I could hardly think at all, could do nothing but sit and wait and endure, desperate to reach home and some kind of rest.

Chapter Nine

It was over a month later that I leaned over a table in my local snooker club, considering my next shot. Jason, from university, had come down to spend a few days with me, and snooker was a good way of passing the time. The hall was dark, almost secretive despite the bright, early August afternoon outside. There were few people around, for it was a Monday, and nobody else was actually playing snooker — the other four men and one woman customer were gathered around the bar, talking genially with the barman.

'The trouble is, I've never been able to think ahead at all,' I said, knocking a red ball three inches wide of the pocket, 'so when I do pot a ball it's very rare for me to continue the break.'

'I just whack the cue ball and hope something goes in,' Jason replied, examining the table. So far, his system had proved the most successful, and he was leading by ten points.

'So, what do you want to do later on?' I asked, as much to put him off his shot as anything else.

'I don't mind. How about going out somewhere in the evening?'

'Sounds good to me. How about going to a little pub near where I live? It's quite nice in there.'

'That's cool.' He blasted the white ball into a group of three reds, scattering the table in a frenzy of multicoloured streaks.

The game progressed for ten minutes as we both displayed an unusual lack of talent, not even experienced enough to claim that the occasional fluke shot was intentional. When, after five barren minutes, Jason sunk a red he gave a cry of surprise and stared at the table as though he could not quite believe it.

'So, when are you heading back to Germany again?' he asked, lining up his next shot.

'I'm not entirely sure yet, I have to book a flight soon.'

'You're flying this time?'

'Yes, I don't think I could stand another epic coach journey.'

'How's the German going?' he enquired, sending a long, straight shot down the table which rolled the black into a middle pocket. 'Eight points, that's our highest break yet.'

'The German? It's okay, I'm still trying to learn.' The green felt of the table was like a reflection of guilty thoughts. I had taken a language cassette from the library but had hardly progressed at all. Every time I sat down with the intention of spending an hour improving my skills, a hundred other pressing issues emerged and the lesson was postponed. Either that or the very attempt at learning German was somehow painful, a vast reminder of our troubles.

'Yes, yes, yes,' Jason watched the red ball roll towards the middle pocket. 'No.' It rebounded from one edge, lying dead in front of the target. I looked towards the bar, noticing that only two men remained besides the barman. They were all at home in one sense, raising glasses occasionally, then settling them with a familiar knock as the numbing liquid dissolved through the taste buds and into the body. A television screen in one corner played the closing sequence of a soap, its characters unnoticed from within.

'Shall we have a drink after this game?' I suggested, desiring to sit and talk for a little.

'If you want, it shouldn't take us very long to finish.' Only one red remained on the table which meant that just seven successful shots were required to complete the match. At that point, however, we both began to play worse than ever, missing everything, ricocheting colours between the cushions with mounting frustration.

'Finally,' I sighed as the last red was eventually sunk. 'Now we just have to pot six more.'

'Or we could give up now,' Jason suggested.

'Or we could give up now.' I examined the table with the six balls lying melancholy along its length, then at the score-board where Jason held a sizeable lead. 'All right then, we'll call it a day.'

We loaded the balls back into their tray and returned the equipment before ordering drinks. It was rare for me to drink alcohol in the day, but I decided to have a beer anyway. Normally I associated drinking in the day with emotional stale-ness, the men and women who have nothing in life but alcohol and spend all the free time that they have in the gradual destruction of their bodies; especially the grey old men who gathered in the bars near my university, gulping away their few remaining years in a fog of memories. Sometimes they seemed so pathetic, and sometimes I realised that they could be happy, but today it didn't seem to matter. I wanted a drink, partly because my nerves were shaking at the thought of our impending visit to the Internet café. Twice a week I would take the bus into town and pay two pounds to use the Internet for half an hour, purely for the purpose of sending an e-mail to Eva, and always I would become increasingly worried as the time approached that she may not have written to me. It was a pointless fear, for I knew that if she hadn't written then there would be a good reason for it, such as a computer failure at her university, but all the same it was a major concern. Only once had I not received a message from her, and the blankness of the screen in front of me had been heartbreaking, to have made the journey expecting to hear from her and finding nothing was like travelling to an oasis in the desert and finding it gone. Returning home horribly frustrated and in a black temper I then had to face the cluttering questions. Why hadn't she writ-ten? Was there a problem? Should I phone her? If I did phone her then would it seem that I was being possessive? I would have liked to have gone to the café as soon as we arrived in town, but it didn't open until late afternoon, and so it was with a troubled mind that I sat at the bar with Jason, trying to make conversation.

'Next week I'm going to apply to join an employment agency, try to find some work for a couple of months,' he was saying.

'That's a good idea, earn a bit of money.'

'Have you ever worked, Dave?'

'No, not properly. I nearly had an interview for a job once.'

'What happened?'

'I applied for a job at a factory last summer, to try to make some extra cash to help me at uni. They wrote to say that all vacancies had been filled, which I was actually very glad to hear, so I booked a short holiday instead, thus spending money instead of earning it.'

'Oh well, you probably had a better time.'

'Probably. The strange thing is though, after I'd booked the holiday I got a phone call from the factory saying that they did have vacancies and would I like to come to an interview, but of course it was too late by that time. Quite a lucky escape really.' I smiled, as it was one of favourite stories for such situations.

We took half an hour to drink our beer, while I wished that we could hurry up and leave, so that at least I would know one way or the other. If only she had written then it could be a very pleasant afternoon. The bar was polished and I slid a beer mat along and back with my fingers. The mat was damp where a glass had recently stood, and I wondered what it had contained.

'Well, we might as well get going,' Jason said, and my heart jerked painfully as it felt as though we were about to ride forth into a desperate battle.

We left the snooker hall, down the rather grimy flight of stairs and out into the busy main street of the town. People strutted along in their summer cloths, each man seeming to compare himself to every other, and I knew that the twenty-minute walk would be nerve straining. Still, it was good to have Jason with me as it could be a very lonely walk, and even though I was still alone with my worries it was at least possible to talk of other matters and expand the world beyond a single issue.

'Have you ever considered getting the Internet at home?' Jason asked as we crossed a road near a petrol station, irritable drivers gurgling fuel into their stinking machines above the baking tarmac.

'It would be useful, but as we get it free at university for most of the year there doesn't seem much point.' A man slammed the door of the house opposite, its brown walls sweltering in the sun and the fumes. As we walked I was surprised by a sudden wave of exhaustion that seemed to grow from within my soul as much as from my body. I felt almost desperate to sit down, as though I could close my eyes and fall asleep right away, but I fought the sensation down and continued.

The road was very noisy, reeking with the venom of the traffic and the modern day. Every driver who passed us seemed to be a little on edge, as if half-aware that something terrible was about to happen, the knowledge of which lay deep within the human psyche.

'This is the kind of day that the world is going to end on,' I said.

'It's so true,' Jason replied, glancing upwards at the huge cavern of sky as if he expected death to come shimmering towards us in the form of a gigantic meteorite or bolt of destructive energy.

Everything was so similar to Eva's university town. The same kind of atmosphere within the scorched afternoon of jagged thoughts, yet it was also different, especially within my mind, as though one town was somehow a reminder of the other, the reality distilled from the dream.

We were approaching our goal now, my heart rate increasing with every step. We crossed another road, devoid of cars but with a feeling of impending doom, the hour filled with danger. *She probably has written, and even if not, there'll be a good reason for it. But if she hasn't, then the afternoon'll be ruined, you won't get any rest until you know.*

Sweating past an advertising board, alongside a parade of run-down shops, Jason saying something amusing that I didn't hear . . . The first sight of the Internet café in the distance, heart pounding . . . *Is it open? Please, it must be open, yes, yes it is, there are people inside* . . . legs weak as I approach the door and, pushing it open with a little force, enter . . .

'I just need to use the Internet for half an hour, mate,' trying to sound calm . . .

'That'll be two pound then.' Musty, carpet smell of the place rushing through my brain . . . Type in the web site . . . it takes an age to load with me quite out of time and space, existing in a different place entirely . . . In pain from the nerves, enter my password . . . can hardly type, watch the screen load . . . Yes! The bliss of relief, of momentary freedom, her name upon the screen next to an unread message . . . almost tearful . . .

'Great,' I said to Jason, unable to hide my joy,' I've got a message from Eva.'

'That's good.'

I glowed for a few moments before opening the e-mail, enjoying the suspense of not knowing what was written.

Hi Dave,

How are things with you? This morning I went early to university to meet my tutor but he didn't arrive, so it was all wasted. I was thinking of you especially yesterday because my mother was talking about the festival and asking what I thought of it. Have you booked any travel yet?

Tomorrow I look forward to a day off, but I will have to spend most of it working anyway.

One important thing that has happened is that I have found a job. I shall begin to work at a furniture store near the university this weekend. It will be every Saturday afternoon, so not too bad. I also met Jens the other day and he said a big hello to you.

I'm really sorry that this is so short but I have to catch a
bus and I fear it might already be away.

So, see you soon,

LOVE
Eva

Sometimes a short message would worry me, but the
word *love*, printed in capitals, was heart-warming. I was lost
for a moment in a deep, tender happiness, a great rush of
goodwill towards the Internet café and its inhabitants. And
Eva had a job. That was neither good nor bad, but certainly
working in a furniture store was better than slaving over the
counter of a fast-food restaurant, struggling to satisfy the
demands of short-tempered customers.

As I began to type my reply, aiming as ever to express my
love without sounding contrived, I found myself yearning
more and more for her to be with me at once. Sitting by my
side, Jason was examining a leaflet about an Internet feature.
He was a good friend, I thought, but it just wasn't the same
without Eva, there was always something missing when she
was not by my side. We had become family, married in a
strange, emotional sense. Nothing would be right until we
were together again.

'What are we going to do now?' I asked after completing
my reply and sending it, relatively happy with what I had
written.

'How about something to eat?' Jason replied, having
made a great show of not reading my message by burying
himself in the leaflet for twenty minutes.

'There's a kebab shop back near the snooker club, if you
don't mind walking.'

'Lead on then. There are few distances that I wouldn't
transverse for a kebab.'

It was a happier walk back to the main street. I was
relieved, and inclined to laugh at just about anything in that
wash of thankfulness. Everything appeared to be far more real

as we retraced our steps; I realised that it was, in many ways, an entirely different world to that which we had passed through less than an hour before. The cars did not roar along in such a hostile fashion, people were vulnerable instead of evil.

The kebab shop was opening as we arrived. It was quite a large place with a dozen red plastic tables and a small television screen mounted in one corner. Beyond the counter were the huge skewers of turning meat and mounds of pita bread.

'I think I'll have a doner kebab, please.' Jason addressed the elderly man behind the counter with some relish.

'Is that small, large or extra large?'

'Extra large? Well, I think I might try that.'

'And you?' the man asked, turning to me.

'How much is a portion of doner meat and chips?'

'Four pounds.'

'Ah.' Rather expensive. I examined the price list. 'I'll have a large doner kebab then.'

'Salad and chilli on both?'

'Salad, but no chilli, please.'

'Both for me,' Jason smiled.

The man heated a couple of pita breads and draped the long strands of meat into them, silver tongs against the grilled brown. The smell filled the room, reminding me how hungry I was. The salad was lifted on and the food handed across wrapped in white, greaseproof paper. After paying, we sat at one of the tables and ate without speaking for a few minutes.

'Enjoying it?' I asked at length, beginning to feel full and slowing my pace.

'Yes, it's all right.'

It reminds me of being at uni.'

The chair was plastic but surprisingly comfortable. I glanced around the shop more closely, noticing the floral stripes of the wallpaper, and then switched my attention to the television which appeared to be showing some kind of documentary. It was not in English so I had no idea as to what was being explored, but what caught my attention was the music, slow and continuous, that played above the speech. Although it was not a German programme, it held for me the distinct murmur of Bavaria, the kind of music that I had heard from time to time muttered by the radio or hauntingly echoing around a festival night, between the beer tents and madness of the previous June. For a moment I was back among the dazzling morning and the drifting, chaotic nights. I thought of mountains, roads, cities of confused life, the same music, ambitions and pain, stretching around eternity, each generation lost in the dreams of others — of our lives reaching out in confusion across the turning years.

> *When spring comes back with rustling shade*
> *And apple-blossoms fill the air —*
> *I have a rendezvous with Death*
> *When spring brings back blue days and fair.*

And I thought of Eva's city, that great unreal sprawl, and of the darkness that had fallen on us during that final riverside walk. The presence of the tower was still strong, bleak and alien, brooding over the skyline before the dead water, beyond grey streets of slouching youths, nettles writhing from the ground, the sky itself a prison. If only Eva were coming to England, then there would be no worries about the real dangers of the city — my fear of violence and the complications of meeting with a foreign culture.

'There certainly is a lot of meat in this kebab,' Jason said appreciatively.

'Are you going to manage it all?'

'I should think so.' His little blue plastic fork lay unused on the table. Jason ate as much as possible with his hands.

'You always were a great kebab fan, I suppose.'

'You're lucky, having a girlfriend in Germany. I hear that kebabs are much cheaper there.'

'I think most of the food is.' I glanced around for a second as a group of three men entered the shop.

'Does Eva still live with her mother?' Jason asked, seeming to read my thoughts. 'Have I asked you that before?'

'No, she's got a place of her own.'

'That's good.' I could tell what was to come next. 'So, how old is Eva?'

'About the same age as us.'

'Ah.'

Why can't you tell the truth? Eva, is this ever going to work? I did not have the strength, I knew, to tell my friend of the age gap between us. It would have been some achievement to have managed it, a way of making the whole issue less important, but it was no good. Would Eva keep her looks with age, I wondered? Not that physical looks were all so important, but in ten years' time she would be practically middle aged. Would she appear middle aged? I tried to picture her at forty, fifty, sixty, twisting my mind to imagine.

And, in the way that all troubles flood the brain at once, the television was suddenly switched to an English channel, probably for our benefit. An advert for some bottled drink was being aired, and the scene was a pulsating nightclub with attractive young men and girls dancing seductively around each other. I watched a stupid-looking man writhe towards a beautiful woman and start kissing her. *My God, Eva goes to nightclubs sometimes, she must meet men like that − Don't be stupid, it's only an advert.* I hated this kind of television − the idea that there is no love in the world beyond sex. I could not stop thinking about Eva in a nightclub. Would she dance with another man if he asked her to? I could almost see it happening in front of me.

'You seem far away,' Jason said curiously.

'Sorry, I was just thinking.' I sought for control, thankful that he had interrupted my runaway imagination. 'When we've finished eating, how about going somewhere for a drink?'

And so the summer continued, between snatches of hope and moments of agonised despair. One of the most positive days occurred around the second week of August, when I went down to the sea near my house early in the afternoon. The air was very fresh and there was a slight tang of seaweed and ice creams, families with small children scrunching across the shingle. It was a good day to be alone, and I sat for a long time on the concrete sea wall, watching the waves rise and hiss inland before collapsing gently into themselves. Everything was peaceful and eternal, the same motions that had been in place for millions of years, and the road ahead of me seemed less dangerous.

For one thing, my flight was booked. Picking a shard of concrete loose with my fingers I wondered how quickly the remaining time would pass. We would be together again in just over three weeks, with me flying from London to Munich at the beginning of September. I would arrive in Germany on a Tuesday morning, and leave again ten days later, on the Friday night. It was exciting, somehow making me feel luckier than the groups of people strolling past. I felt that nothing could go wrong, or at least that I would be able to cope with complications as they developed. It was possible to see a long way out across the water, and I thought how many times further away Eva was, yet for once this wasn't saddening but romantic, thrilling. We would soon be together again, and being apart for the next few weeks would be almost pleasurable as it would be hardship with an end in sight, a period of looking forward to our meeting.

A dog snuffled past, tilting up its head and seeming to smile. There had been a surprising development in the past week; Eva had informed me in an e-mail that she had told her mother about our relationship, had told her about everything, including the age gap that was of particular concern. She had given little indication of how her mother had reacted, but I had the impression that perhaps Eva did not understand her very well, or had at least misunderstood the situation. Whatever the case, I was looking forward to meeting her mother and hopefully becoming known to her family; most importantly it meant that Eva was defiantly serious about our future. I felt embarrassed and a little guilty to think of all the insecurity that I had experienced when trying to judge her feelings.

To improve matters further, Eva's semester at university had finished, so we would have much more time to ourselves.

All in all, I thought, it should be a far more satisfying stay than that of June.

Later on, I decided, I would go and buy a card for her. As well as e-mails, I usually wrote a letter every week, and sometimes it was fun to send something different than a letter written on plain paper. There was a great pleasure in examining the rows of cards in a shop and choosing one that I thought she would like.

I looked forward to that, but there was no hurry. The sea continued to roll against the shore, and for once I was not dreaming of past days but contemplating the future, thinking that perhaps everything would work out after all.

Chapter Ten

The rain crashed down and, although I stood dry under the awnings of the station, it still drenched the soul. It was a miserable evening in early September, summer unsure whether or not to continue, and I could hardly believe that I was on my way to visit Eva again. I checked my watch—ten minutes until the train was due to leave for the two-hour journey to London. Then there would be a night spent at the airport, probably sleepless, waiting for the morning flight to Munich. Dark clouds were scattered far above the small station, somehow they made me feel homesick, the common dread of the traveller about to embark. The end reward of meeting with Eva seemed very distant, beyond the lonely hours of wakefulness, living from thought alone through the black reaches of night.

An old man and a couple of middle-aged American women were waiting at the same platform. I watched them going through the same motions as myself, checking the time every minute or so, glancing around in that strange waiting nervousness, peering intently at the ground to note every cracked stone and every scurrying insect. The rain drummed down in a shaded rhythm, a kind of poetry from the sky.

> *When all the world is old, lad,*
> *And all the trees are brown;*
> *And all the sport is stale, lad;*
> *And all the wheels run down;*
> *Creep home, and take your place there,*

115

The spent and maimed among:
God grant you find one face there,
You loved when all was young.

Far, far above an aeroplane cut its way through a gap in the
clouds, nothing more than a moving point in the heavens,
utterly detached from the world. It was hardly possible to
imagine that there were people up there, that soon I would be
cruising above the earth — the glittering body of the aeroplane
shimmering its image across the speeding miles.

Why couldn't I be waiting for Eva to arrive at the station,
for her to come to England? I was desperate for us to be
together again, but the evening was so drab that it killed any
sense of enthusiasm that I might have held. If only if she were
arriving here we could walk back to my home in the rain and it
wouldn't matter anymore. Instead, the station was the beginning of the journey and not the end, the first hurdle in a long
race. There would be no bed at night, no rest but rather a
creeping tiredness exhausting the mind.

I had made arrangements with Eva to meet her at eleven
o'clock the following morning at a fast-food restaurant in the
Munich airport. My flight was due to leave London at eight
and was set to arrive at around ten, so I imagined that this
would give me enough time. Over the past week, however,
there had been more complications. Eva had told me that her
mother had reached a very poor state of health, which meant
that she was often obliged to spend the nights at her mother's
flat.

'I would feel so guilty if something happened to her
when I wasn't there,' she told me over the phone. 'I was thinking that you could spend the night at Jens's house if I have to
be with her. It probably won't be very many nights, just if she's
feeling ill.'

This was awkward, breaking up the unspoiled time that I
had imagined us spending together, making it harder for us to
relax or plan anything. Still, it was hardly Eva's fault. More of
a problem was her insistence that I stay with Jens if she had to

be with her mother. I suggested that it would be easier if I were to stay alone at her flat, but she was totally opposed to the suggestion. Her views seemed very unreasonable, after all I could hardly inform Jens that I planned to drop in on him for the night whenever necessary, but I hadn't wanted to argue with Eva over the phone, so the matter rested. At least Jens had invited me to stay with him at some point over my visit, so the option was there in case it became necessary.

When the train finally arrived it seemed to be both the only road to happiness as well as the route to all suffering. I climbed aboard one of the long carriages, filled with that sudden insecurity that often occurs at such moments.

'Is this the right train for London?' I asked the American women who were sitting a little in front.

'We hope so,' one of them laughed, 'but you shouldn't ask us, we're foreigners.'

I placed my suitcase on the floor beside my feet, stirring memories of that final, hot retreat across Germany, over two months distant. We pulled away through the town and into the city beyond, smoky buildings on either side, then out into the country for two rattling hours. It was quite a pleasant journey, I spent some time checking my tickets and worrying about the flight and meeting Eva at the correct place, but more often it was hardly possible to think at all as the fading day rushed past and the rain ended. There was a feeling of concealed dread in the carriage, but it was well concealed, still out of reach. A man with a strong Scotch accent spoke into a mobile phone, and families came and left at the several stops as we headed onwards through the quiet evening.

Gradually, tower blocks began to appear, spreading as we passed them, and I knew that we were in London. We took a long time to reach our destination, and it was a morbid view of the city with the cheerless smog of stone and iron, torn across by grimy roads and rusting rail lines; worst of all were dull bushes that had grown up around the wasteland, so polluted and stricken that they seemed more a creation of humanity than nature.

We continued through this barren landscape, passing graffiti-struck walls and tumbling back gardens of collapsed washing lines, before finally arriving at the big, busy main station where the line terminated. Stepping onto the enormous platform was a strange experience, leaving the seclusion of the quiet carriage to be suddenly surrounded by the frenzy of London.

'Will you *hurry up?*' a middle-aged woman snapped at an elderly lady behind her as they passed close by. 'We're never going to make it at this rate.'

'I'm going as fast as I can,' her companion replied, somewhat subdued.

I immediately hurried towards the Underground, as there was a connection to be made with the train that would take me to the airport. As I descended the vast, soulless stairs I noticed that the station was neither friendly nor hostile, but was simply hurry; businessmen, families, singles, all checking times, approaching officials, dragging suitcases. I still felt a little lost and homesick, but there wasn't space to think too much.

The journey through the Underground was easy, just stand with the crowd until a train bustles along, and step aboard. I found a seat, jammed between an Indian woman and a young man with incredibly long hair. His hair was so long that I had to be careful to avoid sitting on it. So many strangers were packed into a small place. There must have been the same mixture of good and bad, happy and lonely, as anywhere else, but here everybody was interesting and no-one seemed aggressive. We rumbled swiftly through the darkness.

'We get off here, daddy?' A small child burbled to his father.

'No, we're off at the next stop.' The man sounded tired, probably a long day out with the young children. In the end they disembarked at the same stop as I did; I was glad to see that I wasn't the only one leaving at that point, in case of the doors failing to open or some other emergency occurring; I wouldn't have to deal with it alone.

Arriving at the correct station, I found the rest of the journey uneventful. My train was already waiting, and left after half an hour with a handful of passengers spread along its length. We sliced through the night and before long reached the airport; I felt the weight of my small suitcase pulling down on my arm as I stepped onto the concrete. There were still eight hours before take-off.

'So far so good,' I muttered, examining a signpost. It was dark now as I walked, the quiet road occasionally rattled by a yellow taxi. A group of about fifteen young Japanese men and women stood around a car, talking quickly. It gave me a certain thrill to be alone and travelling again, but still I could not believe that Eva was waiting for me at the end of it all.

Finding my way into the main building I saw that it was an enormous room, towering ceiling with check-in desks in the centre of the floor and food and drink outlets around the edges. People were packed everywhere; mostly people like myself, looking bored, confused or tired. Luggage piled up, waiting forlornly for distant flights. I worked out that there were still six hours before I could check-in. *Six hours.* My emotions were dimmed; I felt little but the long passage of time ahead. On huge electronic boards were displayed the arrivals and departures, and again I wished that Eva were on her way to meet me, that I were waiting for her to arrive rather than flying out to Germany.

A coffee shop stood in one corner with plastic tables spread out in front of it, most of which were occupied. A drink seemed a pleasant enough way to waste some time.

'Just a coffee, please,' I told the girl behind the counter.

'What type?'

'How do you mean?' I asked stupidly.

'Latte? Espresso?'

'Do you do normal coffee?'

'Yes, yes.'

'That'll do then.' It was the first conversation that I had made in hours, and it wasn't particularly successful.

I sat at one of the small, round tables, watching a group of men who seemed to be about to head off on holiday somewhere. Under the bold electric lighting I sipped my drink, fairly calm, wondering how quickly time would melt away.

After a while a middle-aged man with an impressive brown beard asked whether he could join me at my table as there were no others free, and after a few minutes spent taking brief glances at each other we managed to start a conversation.

'Long wait?' he asked, noticing that I had checked my watch five times in the previous two minutes.

'Six hours. How about you?'

I'll be checking in soon, actually.' He was almost apologetic. 'I wouldn't much fancy spending the night here.'

'No, I'm not relishing it.' The holiday men in front moved off as a body. 'I'm going to Germany tomorrow.'

'Business or pleasure?'

'Pleasure mostly, I hope.' We both laughed. I felt rather flattered that he had thought I might be on a business trip, but there was no reason why not. I could be anyone—in fact, he could be anyone.

'I'm off to Amsterdam,' he said with a gleam in his eye. 'It's a great city, though I'll be working most of the time.' I was going to enquire as to what business he was in, but he continued quickly, 'of course, I should take a proper holiday sometime, see more of the world.'

It was strangely invigorating to be able to talk, yet when he went off to check in, I hadn't learnt his name, and knew that he would forever remain a tiny speak in the corner of my memory.

At the bottom of my cup floated the cold, lifeless muck of the remains of my coffee. All the other tables were occupied and it seemed unfair to keep my seat when so many people were milling around, hoping to find one. I left the coffee area and took a slow walk around the building, past a collection of pulsating gambling machines, around the silent white walls, past a row of pay phones with a girl crying hysterically into a receiver. I began to feel tired, miserable and lonely along with just about everybody around me. For the first time I noticed that every seat and bench in the place was occupied, mostly by sleeping figures spread out in a bizarre search for comfort. As there were no chairs, I sat on the floor against one wall and took a few sandwiches from my hand luggage. Their plastic wrapping felt damp and slimy as I unrolled them, matching my body's crawling sense of uncleanness. I ate a couple of cheese sandwiches but they didn't taste like food at all; my stomach was so troubled that I was not even hungry — just best to eat something to keep a little energy.

And now everything was quiet. There were hundreds of people in the building but nearly everyone was asleep, on the soft chairs in front of me or the hard benches behind. There were bangs and scrapes emanating from some distance away, but most noticeable of all was a barely perceptible continuous mechanical hum, as though we were all under the control of some supercomputer. After a while I lay down on the floor and, using my suitcase as a pillow, attempted to fall asleep. It wasn't much good, the plastic floor was slippery and a constant reminder of where I was, and although I must have drifted very near to sleep at times I remained in a daze during which I did not dream but was not awake enough to think of anything much, though just occasionally I saw an image of the tower with empty skies beyond. It was a very uncomfortable way to lie, but I hardly noticed. Sometimes it felt as though my brain were swimming around inside my head, and occasionally I heard footsteps tap past or a trolley wheel close by, but it all merged into a grey-black blur as a few hours drifted on. By half past five the place was stirring again. Sitting up, I felt my stomach horribly cramped and couldn't face eating anything, so I went into the toilets and washed my face, wondering exactly where I had been for the last hours. It was a strange start to the day, there was no clue as to what the world outside was like, in fact it was not like being alive at all, rising beneath the public announcements and clatter of feet. I was surprised not to feel too sore, though my mind was on other matters as it was almost check-in time and the beginning of the next stage of the trip.

When the plane finally began its nerve-tightening course to the runway there was a noticeable air of relief among the passengers. Although take-off was only delayed by half an hour it had seemed much longer to those of us who had spent the entire previous night waiting. Check-in had been easy enough, eventually moving through to a waiting lounge where people spoke on mobile phones and looked slightly worried. There was, however, more of a business air than I had anticipated among our group, a feeling that was to some extent reflected in my own thoughts. There was still no sense in my mind of a glorious return to Eva, no romantic images of flying back to her. The journey was something that had to be completed, like a business problem that had to be solved, before I could enjoy the real purpose of this effort.

We had remained in the waiting lounge until take-off time, mingling German and English language playing around my ears, and then after boarding there had been another wait which the pilot had apologised for. My seat was next to a window overlooking one wing, and next to me were two German gentlemen with whom I exchanged only a few words as they sat down. Now, as we began to speed down the runway there was an almost relaxed atmosphere, as though flying were an ordinary part of the working week for most people on board. Certainly this was my first air journey for two years, but apart from the build up and the heart-turning moment when we lurched from the ground with the airport diving away smaller and smaller below, it wasn't too dramatic. Airborne, we soon entered cloud and there was no view, nothing to do but sit and wait.

As time passed amid the light chatter, I began to wonder where we were, wishing there were a map somewhere showing our present location. It was hard to believe that we were moving at all until the cloud cleared, and then below there was suddenly an unending mass of fields, lined by tiny rows of hedges, a landscape of differing but gentle colour. I felt for a moment what could only be described as a slight patriotic homesickness, the rolling countryside below that I was leaving behind to explore my dreams in a foreign place.

> *If I should die, think only this of me:*
> *That there's some corner of a foreign field*

That is forever England. There shall be
In that rich earth a richer dust concealed.

There was even a little village, tiny church and scattered cot-
tages, the kind of scene that poetic young Englishmen had
gone to war on in nineteen-fourteen.

Looking over the wing of the plane I noticed that it
appeared to be shaking. Quite normal, I assumed, but what a
bizarre thing we were doing, all suspended above the clouds
in a piece of metal. Human life, so fragile and so determined to
flout this fragility—yet this was not a thought that brought
fear, but rather a kind of drifting peace as there was, after all,
nothing that I could have done in the event of a disaster. The
view misted over again and I began to realise how intensely
boring air travel can be when sitting with strangers. Moreover,
I was surprised by my inability to focus my mind on anything
firm, so that the more I attempted to plan or imagine the coming ten days, the more I was greeted by scattered hopes and
images that were difficult to understand.

So we hung there in the sky, minutes passing with no
clue as to whether we were above land or water, until it was
announced that we would be arriving in twenty minutes and I
knew that we must be well advanced across the continent. In
fact, as we began to descend I realised that the flight had actually taken rather less than the two hours expected. Physically I
was not feeling too bad, considering the recent sleepless night,
and I was cheered by the thought that Eva was hopefully arriving to meet me even as we dived back towards the Earth.

And so, after the decent down shimmering steps, the short,
jostling wait at the passport desk and the collection of luggage
with all that confusion and nerves of suddenly being alone in a
foreign country, I found myself amid the crowds in a huge
complex of waiting areas and shops. It was nearly eleven
o'clock, and I found a signpost which informed me that to
reach the correct fast-food shop I would have to go down a

flight of stairs and through a large courtyard. If anything, the atmosphere was a little more relaxed that it had been at the other various stations that I had visited over the past months. Here, people were not in such a frantic hurry, they did not peer around so nervously nor seem so short tempered. Yet despite this I was very conscious of being foreign, mainly for linguistic reasons, always afraid that somebody was about to ask me for directions or speak to me so that I wouldn't be able to reply. In consequence, I felt like a spy afraid of blowing his cover as I passed between the bags and suitcases and bins filled with burger wrappers.

Following regular signs I left the main building and walked out into an open square. The fast-food restaurant was about a minute's walk across the other side, but I paused for a moment because the scene was so striking. The tall, white walls of the complex surrounded the area, so I felt uncannily as though I were standing within the walls of a medieval fortress. The pavement was of the usual grey-white stone, but seemed damp as though it had recently rained, indeed the sunny weather had a feeling of uncertainty to it. Above, the clouds were motionless but cold, and a short distance from where I stood a group of workmen were fixing together what appeared to be a kind of speaker system on a platform, metal rods clanging in ugly fashion and the men calling to one another. I felt so alien that the whole scene was dank and depressing and unbelievably lonely, and it took some courage to even cross to the restaurant. I shivered, hoping to see Eva waiting inside for me, but through the windows there was no sign of her. Now it was a question of whether to wait inside or out. Inside I would have to order something and perhaps try to speak German, but standing where I was with my suitcase I felt so foreign and conspicuous that I pushed through the door and joined the queue at the counter, taking a ten-mark note from my wallet. If I just bought a coke, I figured it wouldn't be too difficult. Just say 'Coke, bitte.' Was it 'Ein coke' or 'Eine coke,' though? I neared the front of the queue, and one of the serving girls caught my eye.

'A coke, bitte,' I mumbled.

'Sorry, a coke?'

'Yes, please.' It was rather humiliating, but at least I had managed to buy a drink. Eva was nowhere to be seen in the restaurant so I sat down at one of the plastic tables to wait for her, feeling a little concerned though she was only ten minutes late. It was very busy inside, and there were hardly any tables free. Most of the people sitting around me were young, and I imagined that many of them were travellers. I felt uncomfortable in the atmosphere, while outside there was the same bleak scene that I had encountered earlier; even as I scanned the square for a glimpse of Eva I noticed a plastic bag gliding in fits and starts across the paving, evidence that a breeze had sprung up. Another ten minutes passed and I felt increasingly lonely and afraid. If she didn't arrive at all then I had no idea as to what the correct action would be, considering my linguistic defects it would be an incredibly awkward situation.

Just arrive, darling, and everything'll be all right. A further quarter of an hour drifted away, while familiar tunes played on the radio. There was so much English and American music about, the restaurant could have been down any city road in London. My heart was beating fast and my stomach was more cramped than ever, I watched the square almost with panic while other diners came and went about me. She was forty minutes late … perhaps some disaster … but then I saw her familiar figure entering the courtyard from the main building. A happy relief washed through me, as suddenly everything was good again. As she approached I could even recognise the manner in which she walked. I saw her scanning the inside of the shop and she waved when she saw me, heading for the front door. It was all so warm and happy that it made the previous journey seem like nothing, seem like an affair I would undertake every week if necessary, because I realised once again how much we belonged together, how like a marriage it was.

She hurried through the door and into the restaurant, and we hugged each other for a few seconds. It was like energy returning to my soul.

'Sorry I'm late, my train had a long stoppage,' she apologised.

'That doesn't matter, I've just been waiting here with a drink.'

'Anything to eat?' she asked, dropping her bag onto the seat next to mine.

'Are you hungry?'

'Yes, I haven't eaten since breakfast.'

'I haven't eaten all day,' I said, realising that I was famished.

'Shall I go and buy something?'

'All right.' I handed her a couple of ten mark notes. 'Get me anything.'

'Will a burger do?'

'I think it's statutory.'

'Okay then.' She walked back to the queue which was quite long again. I sat and looked at the seat beside me with her bag resting on it. Soon she would be sitting there. The day outside had not changed but it was no longer an alien land. We were together again.

Chapter Eleven

While Eva was queuing I watched the workmen outside, feeling as though I had just woken from a frightening dream.

'What do you think they are setting up there?' I asked as she returned.

'It's probably for the Oktoberfest. It starts soon.'

'Before October?'

'Yes, it's strange, isn't it?'

'Perhaps it used to start in October, then it grew.' I examined the burger that Eva had brought me. 'How much did both meals cost?'

'Just over fifteen.'

'Oh right. Shall I give you some more money?'

'No, it's all right.' She took a bite of her burger, but when I did the same most of the layers of salad and relish slithered out onto the tray.

'Oops.'

'Don't worry,' Eva laughed. Suddenly, I began to laugh as well; I felt a maniac desire to shake with laughter, to throw the mess of salad leaves and yellow ooze onto the floor and dance on them. Thankfully, I suppressed the urge, and Eva went on. 'Are we going to spend the night in Munich or go home today?'

I considered. My initial reaction was to favour returning to Eva's flat, where at least we would be at home and I could be sure of some rest; but then I reasoned that it would be far more romantic to spend an evening and a night alone together, away from her usual life. She was beautiful sitting next to me, and now that we had ten whole days together there was no longer the tense frustration that I had felt towards the end of my previous stay.

'Let's spend the night somewhere here.'

'Okay then,' she gazed through the window for a moment. 'I wonder where.'

'Do you know of anywhere?'

'I have a guide book.' She produced from her bag a colourful guide to Munich and turned to the back pages. 'This is quite up to date, there should be numbers for some youth hostels.'

'Wouldn't it be better to find a cheap hotel or a bed and breakfast place?' A youth hostel was not what I had in mind. That would probably mean separate dormitories for men and women, having to meet a lot of people with whom I could not communicate, rather than spending the night with Eva, quite the opposite of what I was hoping for. 'I mean,' I continued, 'are these hostels going to have separate rooms for men and women, because I'd rather be with you.'

'I'm not sure—it doesn't say here what the sleeping arrangements are. Shall we phone some and see if there's any space?'

'Yes, good idea.' I was suddenly very tired, so tired that I could almost have fallen asleep at the table.

'I think tomorrow I may have to spend the night with my mother,' Eva continued.

'Why?' My heart sunk a little.

'Because I think it would be good to spend some time with her, so she doesn't feel left out.'

'How do you mean?' The remains of my burger were damp and unappealing, but I kept eating.

'I just think I should.'

'Fine. That's all right. When can I meet your mother?'

'This week, if I can arrange it. Would you be able to stay with Jens tomorrow night?'

'Probably, yes, if I phone him.' I was too tired to argue.

'After tomorrow night I won't feel guilty anymore, so we can sleep at my flat then.'

'Okay.'

'So long as my mother isn't ill.'

'Okay.'

The buzz of noise around us reminded me of that final lunchtime of nine weeks past, spent in the canteen of the university with the fear of the journey and our parting ahead. There was an ever-present spark of joy that this was the start of another visit, and despite the problems of where to sleep, I was still happy just to have arrived.

We had both finished our food, and although it was gone midday and I had only eaten one burger since the previous evening, I felt completely full.

'Shall we go?' Eva asked.

'Sure. We'd better try and sort out some accommodation.'

We left the restaurant and walked back across the square to the main complex. It had grown warmer and most of the clouds had dispersed; a middle-aged man smiled at us as we passed him, and everything was filled with the calmness that comes after a storm. Inside, we approached a pay phone, and Eva rubbed a few coins between her fingers.

'I'll try some numbers then,' she said, holding the guidebook open and pushing the buttons. After a short wait she began a conversation, soon hanging up with a shake of her head.

'They're full,' she told me, inserting another coin. 'Actually, I think it's very busy here at the moment, with the Oktoberfest coming and it being tourist season.

As she waited for the call to be answered, I realised that I hoped this second attempt would fail as well. In my present condition I felt that I could hardly stand a youth hostel.

'That one's no good either.' She tried a couple more, each with the same result and always with a surge of relief going through my body upon the report of failure. 'Shall we give up for the moment?'

I suppose the sensible thing to do would have been to have insisted that we tried to find a cheap hotel at once, as the booking situation could only grow worse, but I was exhausted and it seemed such a lot of effort that I agreed to leave it for a while.

'Okay then,' I said, 'we'll try again later. I'd better phone Jens.'

'Do you have his number?'

'Yes,' I grinned, 'you didn't expect that, did you?'

'Well, no. I thought you would probably forget it.' She laughed and was lovelier than ever. I found Jens's number in my hand luggage and passed it to Eva.

'You'd better phone in case his parents answer.' I dialled the number while she held the receiver, and after a few moments I heard the call answered and her ask to speak to Jens.

'His mother's gone to fetch him,' she said, handing me the receiver. There was a pause in which I noticed the various international dialling codes printed on the phone stand, then there was a crackle and Jens spoke.

'Hello?'

'Hi Jens, it's Dave.'

'Yes, I thought so. How are you?'

'I'm pretty good, thanks. And you?'

'Yes, yes, the same as ever. So, how long are you in Germany for?'

'Ten days; I'm going back a week on Friday.'

'Really? Is today Tuesday? Yes, of course it is.'

'So, we should meet sometime,' I said, keeping a careful eye on the timer that was counting down our remaining seconds.

'Of course. You should stay for some nights.'

'Yes. Actually I was wondering if I could visit you tomorrow and perhaps stay for the night. Eva has to be with her mother.'

'Yes, that would be good.'

'Great.' I felt a slight touch of guilt; after all, this was only necessary because of Eva's strange insistence that I should not sleep alone at her flat, but then of course I would most probably have spent a night sometime at Jens's house anyway.

'Could you call me tomorrow then, sometime before you arrive? I could meet you at the train station by the university if you want.'

'Yes, that'd be good. We'll probably return from Munich in the early evening, if that's all right.'

'No problem.'

'I'm almost out of time' — the counter was bleeping — 'so I'll call you tomorrow.'

'Okay, see you then.'

'Thanks. Bye.'

'Bye.'

What a wonderfully easy-going person he was, I thought, replacing the handset.

'Is that sorted out?' Eva asked.

'Yes, we're going to meet him tomorrow evening at the train station by the university.'

'That's good, we can meet there on the way home, then I can take the train on to the city. That means we don't have to leave Munich until tomorrow afternoon.'

I lifted my suitcase from the ground.

'If we're going sightseeing then we should put this somewhere. I don't want to have to lug it around all day.'

'Let's take it to the train station and put it in a locker. That'd be best. Then we can tour Munich.' Eva ran her fingers over her hair for a moment, then turned and led the way through the rush and back towards the day.

We caught a bus to the centre of the city, the rhythm of the vehicle and the colours of moving life outside creating an almost carefree atmosphere, a feeling that all was well in the world. It was not very busy on board but we sat near the back, and opposite I noticed a young boy holding a red balloon, like a figure from a picture hanging on a nursery wall. I could almost hear that Bavarian music — like at the kebab shop — playing in my head, untold enchantment and fairytales but always with that slight unease of childhood.

'I heard on the news about a former stripper from my city who's going to stand for election as mayor for another place,' Eva said after a while.

'Oh right, is that the kind of thing that people around here go in for?' I laughed.

'You shouldn't joke about it.' She paused and twisted her fingers. 'I've been made an offer.'

'What offer?'

'I got an e-mail recently asking me if I wanted to be an Internet stripper on this web site.'

'Wonderful,' I laughed, but then in a horrible moment it struck me that she was serious. 'You got rid of the message, I assume?'

'I could be a stripper on the Internet, it's all completely safe. I'd earn good money from it.'

'Now come on, darling, you know you can't do that.'

'It would be safe. Nobody could touch me because I would just be in a studio.'

'That's not the point. Look, stop joking about this, it isn't funny.' I took her hand. 'I don't want you to think about this anymore.'

'Don't tell anyone, will you?'

'Promise not to think about it anymore?' She removed her hand and stayed silent. I was confused. Surely she couldn't be serious about considering becoming a stripper, it belonged on another planet completely. Yet it left a nasty disturbance in my mind. Again, she was wearing one of her skirts with the big side slit. Was she willing to use her body in that manner, I wondered? Surely not, but somehow the thought would not quite remove itself.

We left the bus at the same stop as everybody else, and stowed my luggage in a locker amidst the roar and echo of the huge train station. We also checked the times for return trains to Eva's city, and found that the last one of the day would leave in the middle of the afternoon, which removed any doubts about our spending the night in Munich. There was a stone floor and our footsteps clanked distinctly against the other noise, and when we left I was glad to escape from the confusion.

'So, where shall we go now?' I asked as we stepped out onto the broad, busy street.

'There's a medieval chapel that I'd like to see,' Eva replied, flicking through her guidebook. 'It should only be about ten minutes' walk away.'

In the end it took us fifteen, strolling in the sun past tall, glaring buildings of centuries worn stone. There were crowds everywhere, hundreds of Japanese tourists with cameras, spilling in groups throughout the wide streets. At one point we passed by the edge of a colourful market and decided to return later and explore it. The afternoon promised to be pleasant enough, though I could not forget the fact that we still had no accommodation for the night, nor our worrying conversation on the bus.

Upon reaching the chapel I was surprised by how tall and thin it was, ancient grey blocks piled high in grim order, now with a ticket stall outside.

'It's three marks each to go in,' Eva said, giving a sidelong glance at the ticket woman. 'Shall we?'

If you want to.' I handed her the money and we each received a little pink ticket. I put the square of card into my wallet with almost total disregard, but then the thought struck me that upon returning home I would almost certainly keep it as a souvenir. It would be a special object for a while, and after many years I would come across it in the box where it was stowed and it would stir a memory of a bright afternoon that existed once for an almost unperceivable moment. It was very sad in a strange way — so long as I stayed with Eva I knew that I would keep all the small things.

We explored the chapel, rough walls and the building gutted so it was hard to imagine that it had ever held a religious purpose. Around the sides there were information boards listing its history, but I wasn't terribly interested, apart from discovering that it had played some part in the religious turmoil of the sixteenth century. In the upstairs room, however, I experienced a deep sense of peace. We were alone, yet the window commanded a fine view of the milling tourists below. I stood watching them for some time.

'I've always liked Calvinism,' Eva said. 'Those ideas have a lot of influence around here.'

It was a casual remark, but it made the dark walls around me suddenly take perspective; they had been here, hardly different, in the sixteenth century when the new light of European thought was struggling against the darkness of its past. What minds had drifted here, what suffering had been witnessed across the decades? Looking over the crowds below I thought for a moment of Calvin, of his belief that God had predetermined those who would be saved and those who would fall. It was all a pointless struggle, generations fighting against a destiny that they could never alter. If that was true, then how many of us could really imagine that we were among the chosen, straining as we are, forever ruined by the chains of human life?

As we stepped outside and headed back towards the market I felt the past dissolve; once more we were firmly in the modern city.

'So, how's the job going?' I asked. 'How's the furniture store?'

'It's okay, I just go there every Saturday for four hours in the afternoon and show people around.'

'Are you going there this Saturday?'

'Yes, I have to. You can come if you want.'

'Well, if that's all right with the management.' I could see the stalls ahead, and it occurred to me that Eva was a tourist here as well; it gave us a certain freedom.

We spent a lovely few hours examining the market, squeezing between the crowds and the stalls, yet it was not so busy as to be unpleasant and there was the warmth of people enjoying themselves. After exploring, we brought some pretzels and ate them in a little garden, somewhat detached from the jostling beyond and very much in our own world. I could have stayed there forever, just making conversation and laughing, hoping that people were noticing us together beneath the pale sky. Boisterous folk music was echoing from nearby and the air held a tang of coffee and earth; for a while it made me feel very awake.

As six o'clock arrived Eva suggested that we go to one of the big beer halls for the evening. This idea made my heart skip a beat at first, with images of burly men dancing on tables, but she seemed to intercept my thoughts and reassured me that it was relatively refined.

'It's for tourists mostly,' she said, 'but for locals also. They serve meals there as well, so it's a bit like a restaurant.'

'That sounds good,' I replied, hoping that she wasn't beginning to find me boring and antiparty.

It required another twenty-minute walk to reach the beer hall. The evening was warm and the tourists were still in dominance, flocking down the old roads in a bright mass. Arriving at the hall we paused for a minute to examine it before entering. It was an impressive building that must have once looked severe, but with the sound of music and voices reaching from within it had become welcoming, giving somehow the impression that both the past and the present were contained within its walls and were both just about the same.

The front door was open, a variety of chalked menus on boards outside, and we passed through an entrance hall and into a huge, hot room, filled with wooden tables. A band played folk music in the centre of the room and the men and women crammed along the tables were eating or drinking or clapping along, and it was all very friendly. Assuming that many of the people here were tourists, I did not feel out of place. Somehow it was a reassuring atmosphere. We found a couple of spare seats near the band, and sat opposite an elderly couple who left after a few minutes. There were big, boisterous-looking men sitting nearby, but for once I did not feel any of the paranoid fear that they were looking at Eva and analysing us. There was a kind of freedom in the air.

Men with trays of drinks walked between the rows, and we bought a litre of beer to share. Looking through the glass I could see tiny bubbles rising and vanishing through the shimmering liquid, something like the turning of generations and drifting of life.

'Beer is eternal really,' I said.

'What?' Eva turned her gaze to the glass. The band finished a piece and everybody applauded.

'I mean, people have been drinking beer for God knows how many centuries.'

'Munich is a good city for beer,' Eva said after a while. 'In my guide it says that Wilhelm the Fifth of Bavaria actually founded the Hofbräu here at the end of the sixteenth century because he didn't like the local beer.'

'That's quite impressive. He obviously had his priorities right.'

It was so loud with the band and the background noise that we didn't talk much, but we put our arms around each other and it was lovely and cosy to be able to sit huddled together amid the heat and smoke and laughter, as though the world were turning without us and nothing else mattered for a while. After twenty minutes a middle-aged couple arrived and occupied the seats opposite us. The man helped his wife removed her coat, and they ordered drinks.

'Are you supposed to tip these people?' the man asked, suddenly glancing across at us.

'You should,' Eva replied, leaning across the table.

'What are those big coins? They're five marks, aren't they?' He spoke with an American accent.

'Yes, or two marks.'

'Well, that should have been enough. The waiter gave me a look as though he expected more.'

'Where are you from?' I asked.

'The United States. We're here on vacation.'

'Whereabouts in the United States?'

'Maryland.'

'Ah.'

'I used to be stationed around here when I was in the army,' he went on.

'So he thinks he knows all about it,' his wife grinned.

'Do you live here?' the man asked.

'No, I'm from England. She's German though.' I pointed to Eva.

'Really?' He seemed surprised. 'I find it easier to understand her accent than yours.'

'Oh great, you speak better English than I do, darling.'

'So if you're from England, how did you get to know each other?' The woman asked.

'We met at university in England,' Eva said. 'I studied there until March.' The man smiled and I wondered what he was thinking.

There was a pause in the music which made it easier to talk, and then it began again and after a while the Americans left. They were a nice couple and it was a shame to see them go, but I was starting to think about accommodation again.

'We still have to find somewhere to stay tonight,' I reminded Eva.

'Yes, I know.'

'So what are we going to do? I really have to get some sleep tonight.'

'Yes, yes, I understand that.'

'What should we do then?'

'We could take a walk and see if we find anywhere with rooms free.'

'Okay then.' It seemed a forlorn hope, but I didn't have the energy to argue. I didn't exactly feel tired; it was more a complete lack of strength, both physical and emotional.

We left the beer hall, and as soon as we stepped back onto the street I felt the change that had come over the area. Whereas before the roads had been thronged with tourists, now in the glow of streetlamps they were busy with partygoers and other nocturnal movers. Groups of men in shirts and pale trousers strutted through the night, intermixed with screaming, giggling girls, already drunk. The atmosphere became menacing; I quickened my pace a little though Eva didn't seem at all concerned.

'We should head towards the train station,' she suggested. 'If all else fails then we can spend the night there.'

'I really have to sleep somewhere with a bed,' I replied, knowing that it was hopeless.

I let Eva lead the way, and we found ourselves on a very wide road, flanked by stern, old buildings. The air was sweet but full of fear. There was a lot of shouting from behind and I turned to see a man reeling down the road, waving a beer bottle and yelling at anyone he passed. My heart quickened in a horrible tug. He evidently had the potential for violence, but we were still a good distance ahead of him so by walking fast I hoped he would not catch up with us.

'It's good you can't understand the things he's shouting,' Eva grinned.

'We'd better keep walking.' I was terribly nervous, desperate that we stay ahead of him, quickening my pace. Glancing behind I saw him threaten a group of young men who seemed to scare him away, after which he swayed into a bench and fell over it. For the moment the danger had passed, but it left my nerves tattered and I was suddenly hoping that we would reach the station as soon as possible, where at least we would be relatively safe.

For ten minutes we walked among revellers, my heart beating fast, until eventually we arrived at the entrance to the station without further incident.

'Well, it looks like we're spending the night here,' I said, beaten.

'Yes, we'll have to make the most of it.' Eva sounded a little guilty, but I didn't blame her; somehow I had always known that we would end up here, ever since we failed to find a room from the airport.

Chapter Twelve

It was difficult to know whether it was night or day inside the station. There were still crowds of people, and we walked under the harsh lights, out to the large open area at the front of the platforms.

'We're not meant to be here without tickets,' Eva said, 'so we just have to hope that no-one asks us.'

We sat down against the wall. It had the makings of a hard night.

'I should phone my mother,' Eva continued, glancing around at the people sitting nearby. 'She mustn't know that I'm spending the night at a station, the shock would kill her.'

'What are you going to say then?'

'I'll say I'm at a friend's house or something.'

'All right.' Again, I would have preferred her mother to know that we were together, but there was no use in arguing.

'Wait here then. I'll go and find a pay phone.'

She stood and hurried away. I glanced around the wide, busy building, the tiled floor seeming to stretch away into infinity. There were quite a few people sitting around, and I wondered how many of them were waiting for trains and how many just needed a place to spend the night.

A train departed and I listed to it rumble away and fade into the distance. A woman pushing a trolley piled with suitcases paused nearby, and then sat down.

'Do you speak English?' she asked, rather nervously, after a few moments.

'Yes, I am English.'

'Oh right. It's impossible to tell where people are from without speaking to them, isn't it?'

'Yes, I suppose it is. So, where are you from?'

'Canada; I'm touring around Europe by train.'

'That must be very interesting,' I said, wondering how she managed with her enormous collection of luggage.

'I run a small business, and this is the first vacation I've taken since I finished college,' she went on. 'It's been about ten years.'

'That's a hell of a long time.' She must be in her early thirties, I thought. Some years older than I had imagined her to be.

'I'm Mary, by the way.'

'Ah. I'm Dave. So, where are you heading to next?'

'Regensburg, if they let me on the train. They said that I hadn't booked properly or something, so there might be a problem. Where are you going?'

'Well, nowhere for the moment. I'm taking a train back to my girlfriend's house tomorrow.'

'Oh right. Is your girlfriend here now?'

'Yes, she's just gone off to make a phone call.' In fact, as I was speaking I could see Eva making her way back towards me. I thought how lovely she looked, how fresh. I felt happy that Mary would see us together.

'I've done it,' she announced, sitting down next to me. 'My mother thinks I'm staying at a friend's house.'

'Well done.' There were a few moments of silence. 'This is Mary, from Canada.'

'Hello.' She and Eva exchanged a few words.

'How did you meet each other?' Mary asked.

'At university in England.'

'I see. And do you both study there now?'

'No, I go to my university at home,' Eva said.

'I see.' Mary checked her watch. 'I think I'd better go and check the train again,' she said, standing. 'Will you watch my luggage for me?'

'Sure.' I watched her walk away towards one of the platforms.

'Doesn't she know if it's the right train?' Eva asked.

'They might not let her on because she didn't book.'

We sat in silence for a few moments.

'You know,' I said, 'it's been six months since we were at university together.'

'Really? Six months?' She moved right up to me and took my hand. 'Time goes quickly, doesn't it?'

'Yes, yes it does.' I held her hand tightly. Mary returned looking relieved.

'It's all right,' she said. 'They're going to let me on.'

'That's lucky, otherwise you would have had to have stayed with us.'

'Well, take care.' She laid a hand on her trolley and muttered, 'Dave and Eva,' as though remembering the names for some future date.

'Goodbye, enjoy the rest of your tour.'

'Bye.' She pushed her trolley towards the train and we watched her pass through the painful electric light and surreal hissing of the platforms.

'You won't tell anyone about my offer, will you?' Eva asked after a while.

'What offer?'

'The e-mail thing.'

'Oh don't start this again, darling,' my heart missed a beat. 'I don't want you to reply to that e-mail.'

'It would be for you as much as me, though.' She lowered her voice. 'I would get paid a lot for Internet stripping, and if we had more money then we could see each other more often.'

'Well, of course I want to see you as much as possible, but there are other ways to make money.'

'Nobody would recognise me,' she tightened her grip on my hand. 'It's only men in America who use the service, and they're not interested in my face at all, only in my body.'

'That's just the point. It's taking advantage of you, it's treating you like an object and not a real person.' My pulse had quickened to a point where it hurt and I felt sick. 'Look, you're not really taking this seriously, are you?'

She did not reply.

'Really, I don't want you to do it.' She still made no answer, and I sat there worrying, wondering whether she was really prepared to use her body in that way. Who were these people who sent e-mails to young vulnerable women, tempting them with money to aid the fantasies of lonely men? It was all about profit, a sickeningly successful case of supply and demand. But would Eva let herself be taken advantage of like that? Suddenly I was not completely sure that she wouldn't. I knew that until she had deleted the e-mail message, I would be unable to relax.

Twenty minutes passed and we both grew very uncomfortable on the floor, watching people roll and slide their luggage in front of us.

'I think we're too obvious sitting here,' Eva said at length. 'Perhaps we should move upstairs; we might even find somewhere proper to sit.'

We both stood. My body ached and my mind was numb. Leaving the platform section, we climbed a flight of stairs to the passenger lounge, but decided not to risk waiting inside in case there was a ticket inspection. A little way off we found an unoccupied wooden bench.

'This'll have to do for now,' I said, sitting at one end.

'Do you want to lay down?' Eva asked.

'No, it's all right. You lay down first.'

She spread herself out over the bench with her head on my lap. After a few minutes I began to wonder whether she was asleep or not. An hour passed and a few people walked by from time to time, but nobody took much notice of us. I wished that the minutes would speed up, would end this awful emptiness that I felt inside me. Occasionally Eva opened her eyes or moved a little. Looking down at her face I prayed that she would never allow thoughts of money to corrupt her, that she would never use her body to try and gain an advantage in life. It occurred to me that our suffering together drew us closer, made me more determined than ever to protect her.

Two policemen walked past escorting a third man. I wondered whether he was in the same predicament as us, whether he was being thrown out.

'Look,' he said, 'pointing at us. 'They've been there for ages. Shall I ask them what they're doing?' The policemen ignored him and continued moving towards the stairs, but one of them glanced at me and smiled a little. He had a kind face. I wondered whether they would return and ask us to leave as well, but they never came back.

I thought of the first few days when Eva and I had been dating, and it seemed a lot longer ago than six months. Everything had been simpler then, but of course we now knew each other far more intensely, so that was better really. There was one day I remembered particularly from those first few weeks, when we had sat together in one of the student bars, holding hands and sipping our drinks. I think it was the first time that we had held hands, and it was very special. Some of my block-mates were sitting at a table nearby, enjoying a quick drink before closing time. The bar lights made reflections on the brown, wooden tables and the liquid in our glasses shimmered. I knew that my block-mates had noticed us, and I was so proud — so happy and so proud to be sitting there with Eva. Even the knowledge that she had soon to return to Germany made everything more romantic at the time. And there was nothing to worry about after we left the bar, just walk back to her home together and arrange when to meet the next day.

I jerked my head up, having fallen momentarily asleep, and in doing so woke Eva as well.

'Sorry, darling,' I apologised, 'did you sleep at all?'

'Not really.' She sat up. 'What time is it?'

'Half past four,' I said, checking my watch.

'We can leave at about half past seven or eight.'

'Okay. We still have a few hours, then.' I found that my right arm was shaking and I could not steady it. There was a set of toilets nearby, so I went in to wash my face. Seeing myself in the mirror I was amazed by what a wreck I looked — my face was particularly bad where I hadn't shaved for two days. I took a toothbrush from my bag and quickly cleaned my teeth, feeling rather foolish and hoping that nobody else would enter. When I returned to Eva there was a man sitting next to her, talking. He looked slightly under forty years, and had a rough face.

'Hi,' I said, approaching. He smiled back at me and then continued to talk. I sat on the other side of Eva, and began to feel concerned. I had no idea who he was, or what they were saying to each other and I could not think of a single comment to make to put myself into the conversation. Cursing my inability to speak German, I listened to them talk for twenty minutes. There was something in his voice that I didn't like.

What's he saying to her? They're laughing together. Is he trying to chat her up? You have to think of something to say — but what is there to say? What's he talking about now, why is he pointing? Damn, he's lighting a cigarette, that means he's staying longer. She's bored with me and now she's talking with him.

My hands began to tremble. It was as though I didn't exist at all. It was agonising. Time seemed to have stopped moving altogether and there was nothing I could do to help myself. I was too tired to think of anything intelligent to say that might have included me in the conversation, my brain was too confused.

Eventually, the man checked his watch, said goodbye, and left.

'Who was he?' I asked.

'He's a travelling salesman, or something like that,' Eva laughed. 'He's crazy, he said I should go with him on the train.'

'What?' So he really was trying to chat her up, and I had just sat there and listened to it. An electric shock ran down my spine — I could feel the remains of my confidence dissolving. Suddenly the man appeared at the top of the stairs again. My heart jumped. He handed Eva a piece of paper, said a few words, laughed, and departed.

'That's sweet,' Eva smiled, 'he's given me his phone-number.'

'What? You let him give you his number?'

'Well, I don't want it.' She tore it up and threw it into a bin.

'I don't believe you took it.'

'Oh come on,' she was suddenly angry. 'It doesn't matter.'

'Well, it doesn't make me feel very special, having you take men's numbers as though you're going to call them.'

'What does it matter to you?'

We were both shouting now, just standing in the train station at five in the morning, yelling at each other. Suddenly we were both silent, and I think we both felt very stupid.

'I'm sorry, it doesn't matter.' I pulled her back down onto the bench and put my arm around her. She didn't move away, but she was still angry and upset. I was upset as well. The worst of it was that we had an argument at all, but it hurt me to think that she had given the man the impression that she would phone him. Suppose they met again one day? But no, it wasn't really that fear — more that we seemed to be living in a world of predators where nothing was safe.

More hours went by and we didn't speak much. Eventually, a kind of morning arrived and the people who passed us looked more awake, as though they had enjoyed a night of sleep.

'Shall we get some breakfast?' Eva suggested.

'All right.' We were both subdued, there was a silence between us that was difficult to break. We left the station and walked out onto the already busy roads, traffic cutting through the morning with a business air, almost comforting after the terrible night. We found a fast-food place that had just opened and climbed newly scrubbed stairs to a seating area. The young man behind the food counter looked half asleep beneath the plastic fronted price lists and special offers. Seeing the price of a cup of coffee listed in marks, it occurred to me how these little things make a place foreign, or at least remind us that a place is foreign.

Eva went to the counter and bought us each a croissant and a plastic mug of coffee. The mug had a warning printed on it that it contained hot liquid. I ate the food, but it didn't seem to taste of anything. We sat by the window with a view down onto the road below, to where a few passers-by with bags or briefcases moved along the cracked pavements and birds fluttered between dark buildings. It was a curious morning, the weather neither warm nor chilly, the sky a little overcast. From somewhere out of sight, against the rumble of traffic, I could hear voices calling to each other.

'What time should we head back home?' I asked.

'If Jens isn't expecting you until the evening then there's no point in leaving yet.' Eva swilled her coffee around inside its mug.

'You're right, I guess.' It didn't seem like a good idea to catch a train too soon. I felt that, were we to remain in Munich a little longer, we might be able to re-gather ourselves and make up for the night. Once we arrived back at Eva's home there would be other people to meet, and I would have to go with Jens.

'We could look around the city some more,' she continued, 'and later on we can see the glockenspiel on the town hall.'

'What's that?'

'It's a big clock with moving figures. It plays three times a day, I think. ' She produced the guidebook and flicked through it for a few moments. 'Yes, it plays at eleven, twelve and five o'clock.'

'Well, that should be interesting.'

We sat there drinking our coffee for a long time, and when the last few drops were cold we both pretended that we had not quite finished so that we could sit there for longer. The city continued to move outside, while inside the tables behind us grew busier and a girl joined the man behind the counter. Somewhere in the distance an engine roared.

Eventually we left the restaurant and spent most of the morning walking the streets, crossing dangerous roads, feigning interest in old buildings and famous sights. My feet and legs grew tired but we had to keep walking because as soon as we stopped I began to feel faint, as though I were in danger of falling asleep at any moment. We both knew that the sensible thing would be to head home right away, but neither of us was inclined to suggest it.

'It's eleven o'clock,' Eva said as we stood outside the doors of a museum and decided not to enter. 'Let's start walking back to the town centre for the glockenspiel at twelve.'

We turned along the side of a busy road, past a parade of shops. We were beginning to talk a little more freely and for a while I thought that some of our earlier warmth was returning, but it was no good. Suddenly there was an engine roar, and a man of about twenty-five years sped past in a car and tooted the horn at Eva. She waved back half heartedly, embarrassed. I was falling apart. *Does every man in this city find her attractive? Does this happen every day when you're not here – any lonely traveller chatting her up, any fool with a car honking at her? Yet it shouldn't matter because she loves you – yes, but it does matter.*

I looked at Eva and felt more than ever that we were married. We belonged together, but nobody else seemed to understand.

By twelve o'clock we had reached the Marienplatz, the pedestrianized centre of the city. Once again we were amid crowds of tourists, in and out of huge shops along the wide street. We strolled up to where the crowd was thickest, in front of the town hall where the glockenspiel was mounted. It was an impressive sight; Eva had told me that the building was only one hundred years old, but it felt far more ancient than that, with the Flanders-Gothic architecture looming down mysterious and frightening. It seemed to contain something of the spirit of the centuries, endless hours passing away forever across the Bavarian roads. Above, the sky was growing darker. We stood, staring up at the clock, waiting for it to begin.

'The clock doesn't actually make the music anymore,' Eva said. 'The bells have been replaced by a tape.'

'Really?' I wondered how long the original bells had been meant to last for.

After a while the music started and dancing figures began to move on the glockenspiel. Eva had told me earlier that this was the Cooper's Dance, originally held in the Marienplatz to celebrate the end of the plague. The figures moved with the haunting music—it was like something from a fairground, something from a childhood dream.

The dance had first taken place almost five hundred years ago. What was Eva's city like then, I wondered? Again, it was painful to think that, had I been here five hundred years ago, I could have walked the length and breadth of the country and never found her.

Then, as the crowd stood in thought, the next part of the display began with the models of jousting knights, swinging on their bases, commemorating a tournament that had taken place in fifteen sixty-eight. I was reminded of the pieces of a chess set, particularly of the first time I had ever seen chess men, set out in a shop window one school holiday when they seemed so dark and mystifying. Suddenly, I saw in my mind an image of a similar glockenspiel on a much smaller scale, in a child's bedroom of one hundred years ago. It stood on a table by the bed, long before Eva had existed—and I knew that the child would have grown, lived and died in a world without her. Countless generations had existed before us, knowing nothing of our struggles, rising and falling, full of memories which were now forever lost.

And then, while the music continued, a strong breeze picked up and swept along the street, stirring discarded plastic bags like murmuring spirits; and with that breeze the summer was over—within an instant it was far away and we stood beneath a cold autumn sky of gloomy clouds. And as the eyes of the crowd remained fixed on the moving figures, we were no longer in the present, but a part of an age long ago. The grey, overhanging buildings, the fluttering black birds, the aching clouds, all belonged to the sixteenth century, from when the sounds of the real tournament had rung here. The cold stone beneath our feet echoed to the footsteps of peasants as they trudged on through the bleak harshness of their lives, rain welling between the pavement cracks, men and women returning to their homes in old, dark Europe.

The music continued and I knew that I was looking not at the sights around me but straight into the hidden places of my own mind. And so, glancing at the weary, fragile people around us, I seemed to see before me the figure of a man in a black coat, facing away from us. For a moment I was a part of him, as though the devil himself had entered my soul to witness the icy depth of humanity. And there was a strange comfort in him standing there, but after I had turned my gaze away for a moment and looked back again, he was gone, and just a feeling of abnormality remained that did not fade at once.

'Shall we move away in a bit?' I asked, taking hold of Eva's arm.

'If you want. It's just about finished.'

We crept out behind the crowd and into a quieter part of the street. I kept my hand around Eva's arm, unsure as to whether it was through affection or a childish need to be protected.

'We should find somewhere to eat,' I said, starting to feel a little less odd.

'Are you hungry?' she asked.

'A little. Are you?'

'Not really.'

'Well, shall we just find somewhere to get a drink?'

'All right.' She led way towards the shops. I felt a little more awake and was desperate to sit somewhere where I could regroup my thoughts.

In the end we bought a meal at another fast-food place and sat inside for a long time. It was pleasant to be able to talk, and I felt that we managed to make up a little for the previous night. After spending over an hour inside we went back to the station but found that the next train we could catch did not leave until six o'clock. Having another four hours to waste was a big setback as I was hoping to reach home as soon as possible. In fact, I was in favour of just waiting at the station where we could at least rest a little, but Eva wanted to go out again, so after phoning Jens and arranging to meet him at nine o'clock we set off to explore Munich further. At four o'clock, as we stood in a dark street, it started to rain.

'Bad weather,' Eva exclaimed, glancing at the sky as the first drops fell. 'We should go inside somewhere.'

'Where though?' I peered up and down the road. We didn't really know where we were; both exhausted and wishing we were home.

'Let's go in the church.'

I glanced across to where Eva was pointing and saw that, indeed, a church stood a short way off on the other side of the street. It was half hidden between other buildings, but upon climbing the wet, cold steps and going inside, we found that it was a very large place, a spacious nave surrounded by lofty walls, and quite busy with a service in progress. Several other people entered with us, and we sat at a pew near the back, next to the aisle.

Time passed and somebody at the front was speaking, though I had no idea what was being said. Glancing around, I noticed a series of pillars around the church, some of which had notices stuck to them. The ones nearest were covered in scratches and marks, and I wondered how old they were. The speech continued. I noticed a tramp lying asleep on a pew a few rows in front of us. He was dressed in ragged clothes of various colours and had a bottle full of liquid, which appeared to be tied to his arm. Suddenly everything was very damp and hopeless. I felt like a tramp myself, sheltering from the cold, no idea of what was happening. As minutes went by I began to fall asleep myself, drifting into a half dream for a moment and then jerking awake. I tried to pull myself together, and noticed that the people addressing the congregation appeared to be moving around the church.

'What are they doing?' I whispered to Eva.

'I think it's supposed to recreate Christ's journey to the cross,' she replied vaguely.

Looking around, I noticed that a lot of people were coming and going, as if they had just dropped in to listen for a while. I was going to ask Eva about this, but she had started to fall asleep as well, her head slowly dropping and then jerking up again. They were carrying candles around the front of the church and reciting, and I began to feel nervous, a slow panic rising inside of me. I did not understand the ritual and it seemed almost demonic—with Eva half asleep I was very alone, alone in this old, damp city.

The tramp in front of us awoke and swore loudly. I realised that the people sitting next to Eva were looking at her with some concern, so I took hold of her arm to wake her.

'Shall we leave?' she suggested, heavy lines around her eyes.

'We'd better, before the tramp becomes violent.' It was such a relief to have her with me again, part of me wanting to hold onto her for warmth, to make the day less frightening.

After leaving the church we headed straight back to the station and waited the remaining hours after retrieving my suitcase from the locker. We sat on a bench at the platform, and again I felt much more awake. I put my arm around Eva's waist and she leaned back against me.

'So, I'll be able to meet your mother soon?' I asked.

'Yes.'

'I want to, you know. Because I want everything to be right between us.'

'Yes, so do I.'

'So when we arrive at the university station, I'm going home with Jens and you're going to take the train back to your mother.'

'Yes, then I can try and arrange a meeting time.'

It was very cosy on the platform and I was a little disappointed when the train finally arrived. Few people boarded, so we were alone in our small carriage. As we pulled away with the comforting rhythm of the passage, I knew that one issue in particular was still nagging at my mind.

'Eva?'

'Yes?'

'You're not going to reply to that e-mail, are you?' My heart rate quickened as I asked the question. Suddenly a horrible possibility entered my mind. 'Are you?'

No reply. After a minute I put my arms around her.

'What's the matter, darling?' I asked. She said nothing, but leaned back close against me. 'Eva, you haven't already replied to that message, have you?'

She made no answer.

'Have you?'

'Yes.' She paused. 'At first it was just something to do.'

'How long have you been doing it for?'

'A few months.'

'Oh God, Eva.'

'As I say, it's all safe because it's in a studio. And I get proper training.'

'Proper training? Darling, haven't you thought how this makes me feel?'

'It's just lonely men in America. Most of them want to talk most of the time, over the Internet, to find out all about my life. They're just lonely.'

'You don't understand, do you!' There were tears running down my face but I didn't care.

'It's good money,' she went on, 'and I get extra per minute if I get them to stay and talk.'

'You sound like a—,' I nearly said *prostitute*. 'You sound like you don't care anymore.'

She did not reply and we sat in silence for a minute.

'Eva, you know I'm upset about this,' I continued slowly, 'but it doesn't change the way I feel about you. Not at all.'

No answer.

'I mean, I do think we have a good future together. Don't you agree?'

Silence.

'Don't you?'

'No,' she said at last.

'Why not?'

'I have to look after my mother.'

'Yes, but that doesn't matter to us, does it? It's great that you want to help your mother, but you can't let it spoil your whole life.'

'My whole life?'

'You know what I mean.' We both fell silent. There seemed to be nothing more to say.

The train continued to cut through the evening. I let go of Eva and dried my eyes. I wondered what happened next, but was too tired to focus my brain on anything much, to consider whether she really saw no future for us or was just tired and fed up, and whether it made any difference now either way. I was angry with Eva, but most of all I was angry with the people who had sent the e-mail out in the first place, for they were the ones taking advantage of her. I wanted so much to do something to help her, to help myself, but there was nothing that could be done, no point in arguing further. We spent the rest of the journey in silence, not even looking at each other. I had no idea of what would happen when we arrived at the university station. As the train began to slow I felt a shot of nerves.

'Better get our stuff then,' I mumbled.

'Yes.'

I took my suitcase and we climbed down onto the platform. Almost at once I noticed Jens, waving from his car.

'There's Jens,' I said, pointing.

'Well, goodnight then.' Eva began to move off towards the station. Jens climbed out of his car and called to us.

'Hi.' I walked over to him awkwardly. The air was cold and I felt like my heart was collapsing through my stomach.

'How are you, Dave?' Jens asked, glancing across at Eva who was walking slowly away.

'I'm okay. Excuse me for a moment.' I hurried after Eva and caught up with her just outside the old, white station door.

'We haven't arranged a place to meet tomorrow,' I said, my voice weak. I was terrified of what she might say, but she said nothing, so I continued, 'I'm sure everything'll be fine, we just have to make some effort.'

'Yes, but when are you going to meet my mother, and where and how?'

'I don't see what's so difficult. Why don't I see her tomorrow?'

'I don't know, it might be all right.' She was begging to sound angry.

'So, where shall we meet tomorrow?'

'I don't know.'

'How about at the station in the city?'

'Okay.'

'We'll meet at one o'clock on platform five, at the city station. Is that all right?'

'Yes.'

'Right.' I turned away, too confused to know what to think. Just platform five, the city station at one o'clock. Retracing my steps I found Jens waiting.

'We have to hurry,' he said. 'I'm not supposed to be parked here.'

'Let's go then.' I climbed into the passenger seat. Jens looked at me for a moment.

'Are you okay?' he asked.

'Yes, I'm fine.' Poor Jens, I thought, I'm always messed up when I see him these days.

'Eva's going home by train, is she?' he asked, swinging the car away.

'Yes, that's right, she'll be fine. Anyway, how are you these days?'

'I am extraordinarily well.'

'That's a relief.' We passed though the quiet roads, the rhythm of the car almost sending me to sleep. 'I haven't slept for sixty hours,' I said.

'Really? You'd better go to bed at once. Why have you not slept for so long?'

'One night at the airport and one at the train station,' I replied, shivering. My soul was numb.

'My parents have gone out for the evening,' he informed me as we arrived at the house and he unlocked the front door. 'Would you like anything to eat?'

'Yes, please.'

We sat in the kitchen and ate some bread and cheese. I found that I could barely sit still; my legs seemed to be moving of their own accord.

'Would you like a shower before going to bed?' Jens asked as we finished.

'Yes, I think I'd better.'

He found me a towel and I went down into the basement to the shower room. I could hardly remove my clothes and my feet slipped on the plastic tiles. The water was quite cold, and I noticed a large spider sitting in one corner, but nothing mattered anymore. I felt like my body was covered with seaweed.

It's over, isn't it? You can't split up with her yet, you haven't even kissed her properly. It's no good anymore – she's fed up with you. But she's exhausted as well, not thinking – but how can you carry on now, knowing what you do know?

I was half convinced that I had to end our relationship, yet at the same time terrified that she would want us to split up. Vaguely aware of water running over my face I realised that I felt inferior to Eva, at least in a physical sense. She was so perfect, so totally attractive to me that I doubted I would ever find anyone like her again. I felt so small and weak; part of me doubted that I would ever want another girlfriend. I could not imagine ever loving anybody else.

After a few minutes I turned off the water, dressed and went back upstairs. Jens showed me up to the same room that I had occupied on my previous visit.

'Well, goodnight,' he said.

'I'm sorry I'm so tired. I'll be better tomorrow.'

Don't worry. You've had a long day.' He closed the door, and I stood for a few moments looking at the bed before changing.

The night was heavy outside, and when I climbed into bed I did not fall asleep at once, as I had expected. Rather, my mind gradually dimmed until I sank into a darkness that was devoid of dreams.

Chapter Thirteen

There was a cold feeling to the room when I awoke the next morning. My legs felt very weak; I groped around for my watch and discovered that it was only just past eight o'clock. I had imagined that I would sleep for much longer, but then the whole pattern of sleeping and waking was confused.

Sitting up, I glanced around the familiar room. The woody smell was particularly reminiscent of my earlier stay, and nothing seemed to have changed. The portraits on the wall stared back at me, and I lay down again and tried to consider the events of the previous day. It occurred to me that the sense of unreality that had haunted me in Munich and before had greatly receded. Now everything was cold and clear and I was firmly in the present, yet a part of me could not believe what I had discovered.

So she was an Internet stripper, she had been doing it all through the summer months as I longed away the days until we could meet again. And what happened next? To split up with her would be to destroy all my hopes, leave me with a mess of painful memories and broken desires, yet to try and continue with the knowledge of what she was doing—

Should I try and live with it, I wondered? Say, 'Eva, it's your choice, and if you want to do this job then I'll just have to learn to accept it'; tell her that it's her own responsibility? But no, it would never work, I could not accept it. It was just too horrible. I could even imagine what happened: One of the subscribers in America would log onto the web site and perhaps he would see a gallery of different available girls, then he would select her and she would do her strip for him, after which she would try and get him to talk with her over the Internet, the whole time earning more money. God, I felt so sick to think about it. It was like she was a prostitute — men would actually choose her to —

My head was swimming again. I had no idea how she would react when we met each other, whether she would even turn up, yet there was a certain peace in this, the feeling that events were begging to turn beyond my control.

After a while I dressed and opened the curtain. That dazzling summer view had gone now, but the fields were still gentle in the early autumn breeze. I went downstairs and found Jens and his mother in the kitchen.

'Morning,' I said to the room generally.

'Did you sleep well?' Jens asked.

'Yes, thanks. And you?'

'Yes, perfectly.'

'Splendid.' It was warm in the kitchen, and seeing an everyday breakfast scene around me was like stepping back into normality. I had been so used to mixing with travellers over the past few days that it was a relief to have arrived somewhere.

I ate some more bread and cheese for breakfast, and the three of us sat around the table and talked as best we could.

'What time are you going to meet Eva?' Jens asked.

'I said I'd meet her at one o'clock at the city station.'

'I can give you a lift there if you like.'

'Thanks, that'd be useful.' It occurred to me that I should not put Jens to too much trouble on my part, so I added, 'In fact, if you just take me to the university station then I can take the train from there. That would save you having to drive to the city.'

'All right then, if you're okay on the train.'

'Yes, I should be.' Odd that the prospect of making the short train journey on my own was not at all worrying. On my previous trip I would have dreaded having to travel alone for any distance.

Anyway, I spent the morning with Jens and we watched television and talked for most of the time. It was relaxing, and I didn't think too much about Eva and our troubles. I spoke with Jens's parents a little and we had a happy few hours. Just after twelve o'clock, having eaten a small meal, we drove back to the university station.

'How many stops do I have to wait?' I asked as we pulled up in the car park.

'I'm not sure,' Jens said. 'Probably just two or three, but it'll be obvious when to get off.'

'Hopefully so. Well, doubtless we shall meet again sometime over the next week.' I had no idea when we would meet again, what would happen with Eva. I wondered whether I would need somewhere to stay sooner than he imagined.

'Yes, phone me sometime.' I slammed the door shut and he drove away and left me feeling rather guilty, wishing that I had firmer ideas about what the future held.

The train journey went very smoothly. I checked the times on one of the boards and found that it was a fifteen-minute ride, so by timing the trip I could be fairly sure of disembarking at the correct station. I bought a ticket from the machine, and gazed upward for a moment, noticing the calm skies. Waiting on my own, I did not feel like an alien. For once there was no sense of being conspicuous, no fear that I was obviously foreign. There were quite a few people on the platform, but when the train arrived there was no difficulty in finding a seat, and it was almost pleasurable to be riding alone. We passed through the town and out into the cooling countryside, and my worries were so detached that I felt like a businessman on his way to deal with a difficult client. Still, when we arrived at the main city station and I stepped down onto platform two, I knew that the next hours would not be at all easy. Somehow I had to talk with Eva about what was happening, about what we wanted to happen in the future.

Platform five, we had said. I stood for a while before descending the stairs, noticing how the day was growing warmer. A feeling like tiredness was creeping over me, a very sad feeling, but it faded as I walked down to the passageway connecting the platforms. The time was one o'clock precisely, and when I arrived at the top of the stairs I saw that Eva was already there. She was standing some distance away, looking in the opposite direction, and I stood watching her for a while. The sun was warm and mysterious, and I knew that I would never really be able to understand the situation—all I knew for sure was that a part of me wanted to walk away and leave her there, but after a minute she turned and saw me.

'Hello,' I said. 'How are you?'

'I'm all right. Did you have a good trip.'

'Yes, yes.' Jens gave me a lift to the university station and I caught the train from there.'

We stood in silence for a few moments. I had the impression that she was about to say something important, but she did not speak. We were alone on the platform with the sun on our backs and everybody else seemed a long way away.

'Shall we get a drink somewhere?' I suggested eventually.

'All right.'

We walked back to the main part of the station and sat in a half full coffee bar at a table for two. It was quite a grotty room, the walls were dark and there was dirt on the floor, but the coffee was fine.

'So,' I said, after we had been sitting for a few minutes, 'what are we going to do today?'

'I think you should come and meet my mother later on.' So that was it then, we were continuing. I knew then, in an instant, that we would not talk about our other problems that day—I loved her so much that I could not find it in me to raise the difficult issues, now that we were together again.

'I told her that we would visit her at about four o'clock, if that's all right,' she continued.

'Yes, that's fine.'

'So we have a few hours to spare.'

'What do you want to do?' I turned the cup around in my hand.

'We could go for a walk. There's a big park just by here which is nice.'

'That's sounds like a pleasant way to waste a few hours.' It was still impossible for me to focus my mind. The long-term world hardly existed, and we were just two people sitting in a coffee bar. We were sitting in a coffee bar but somehow I knew that it was not right.

We spent two hours in the park near the station, strolling hand in hand between the flowers and the water features. We didn't talk much, but we watched the children out with their parents and it put me in mind of my own childhood, of days when I had run around in parks and hunted through the long grass. I must have seen many couples walk past then, grown-ups holding hands and keeping to the paths. I felt happy to be with Eva again, yet at the same time the thoughts of my child-hood disturbed me. It seemed that I had always known that I would end up here, in this park on this afternoon. That even when I was very young I had sensed that Eva was waiting for me, and that I had waited all my life to find her.

'We should have gone to the zoo,' she said as we paused to examine a rock garden.

'Well, we've still got over a week to go.'

'Are you coming with me on Saturday, to my furniture store job?' she enquired.

'Yes, if that's all right.' I was pleased that she had asked. 'Are we going to stay at your flat tonight?'

'Yes, I suppose so,' she glanced across at an old picnic bench. 'Shall we sit down for a bit?'

We sat next to each other on the bench, and after five minutes had passed I tried half-heartedly to begin a serious conversation.

'So,' I said nervously, 'did you enjoy our visit to Munich?'

'It was all right.'

No good. It was too pleasant in the park to discuss our problems, however much they were hurting me. I thought for a moment of the dark city tower, of the bleakness that sur-rounded it.

'Eva, have you been down by the river recently, you know, where we went for a walk on my last evening in July?'

'Up by the old bridge?'

'No, further on than that. Where there are those tower blocks across the water.'

'No, I've not been that way recently. I've got no real reason to go there.'

'I see. Eva?'

'Yes.'

'I'm looking forward to meeting your mother.'

'I think she's looking forward to meeting you.'

'That's good. Just you'll have to translate everything.'

'Yes, she doesn't speak English.'

There were suddenly a lot of people walking nearby us, people of all different ages. Strange to think that most of them would not remember this particular afternoon in the park, and yet their lives would forever contain these moments, as though they bound us all together. Time was passing and our lives were slipping away, one autumn would soon be another as we grew older.

'Eva?'

'Yes?'

'I do love you, you know.'

'Yes, I love you too.' She put her arm around me, and she was so wonderful that I almost cried because things were not right.

At half past three we caught a bus through the city to Eva's mother's flat. I recognised a few of the roads vaguely, but the street that we disembarked at, despite being only ten minutes' walk from Eva's flat, was completely new to me. It took us two minutes to walk to her mother's flat, and on the way we passed a restaurant half full with diners. Still, I found it hard to believe that anything was real, as though the restaurant and the people inside were part of a dream, that as soon as I returned home they would all dissolve. It was a warm evening, and it occurred to me that the sense of unreality seemed to be brought on by the heat.

I think we both felt quite nervous as we approached one of the big, dark buildings, up a short flight of stairs to where a row of buttons was mounted beside the main door. Each button had a name below it, and Eva pressed one and spoke for a few seconds through a device in the wall. A female voice answered.

'It's so my mother knows it's us,' Eva explained. She opened the front door and we entered a narrow corridor. A passageway ran to the left and the right, and in front there was a flight of stairs. The overpowering first impression I gained was of a distinct smell of staleness, difficult to describe, but it made me wonder what it must be like to live there.

We turned left and passed one door, before Eva knocked on the second. There was a pause of about five seconds, and then her mother opened the door and smiled at us. I was surprised by her appearance, she did not look at all as I had imagined she would; a tiny woman, perhaps just two-thirds her daughter's size, her face so deeply wrinkled that it seemed to have no clear shape, and her eyes sunken but kindly. We shook hands, and she said a few words to Eva, as though verifying my identity, and then we all went into the flat and sat down. It was much more pleasant inside than out, there were interesting paintings on the walls and magazines lying everywhere. I sat a little awkwardly on the big sofa, Eva next to me and her mother in an armchair.

'My mother wants to know if you can speak German,' Eva said.

'Tell her no, but I'm learning.' The message was conveyed and the mother smiled and said something else.

'My mother says that you have to learn German, because she's too old to learn English,' Eva translated.

And the whole matter of language was a crazy thing. We sat there for an hour, talking ragged, unsatisfying sense, unable to progress beyond the basic questions of family, education and travel. At one point, Eva went out of the room to make tea, and while she was gone her mother spoke to me in German.

'*Wie bitte?*' I didn't have a clue what she had said, but I asked her to repeat it anyway. She spoke more slowly but I still couldn't follow her.

'*Ich verstehe nicht,*' I apologised. Suddenly she started to laugh. Eva returned, and when her mother spoke to her, she began to laugh as well.

'She asked you whether you could understand her,' she told me.

'Ah, sorry.' It was quite embarrassing, really; but I was very happy to have met Eva's mother, and as the minutes passed and we sipped our tea I felt that I had achieved something to be sitting there, an accepted part of Eva's life, visiting her mother's flat. She seemed like a nice woman, not happy as such, but friendly enough. I wondered how old she was; surely not much beyond her mid-seventies, though of course she was ill. In fact, the more I thought of it, the more I could sense illness in the room, a well-hidden breath of decay, lurking behind a wall hanging or under a vase.

After a while Eva told me that it was time to leave and we walked to the door.

'My mother says that she looks forward to having a good talk with you when you are able to speak German,' Eva said.

'Thank you, hopefully it won't be too long.' We shook hands again, and I followed Eva back down the corridor and out into the street.

'Well,' I said, after we had walked for a minute, 'that all went pretty well.'

'Yes, I suppose so.' There was a peculiar note in her voice.

'Anyway, I'm glad to have done that. Perhaps we'll see her again over the next week.'

'We might.'

It did not take us long to reach Eva's flat, and arriving back at her road, then climbing the stairs and walking into her sitting room brought a string of familiar glimpses and smells, so that it was almost like returning to the previous June. But, as I glanced around and noticed that nothing had changed, I felt wonderfully free of that sense of persecution that had haunted me before, as though some dark spell had been lifted.

We had tea in the kitchen, and watched a little television. Several times I tried to gather enough courage to raise the subject of her Internet job, but it was no good; I wondered when the right time would arrive for such a conversation, but surely not on our first proper evening together. Anyway, what happened on that evening took me completely by surprise, and, had she not obviously been prepared for it, I would have imagined that it took Eva by surprise as well!

We were sitting together on the sofa, talking about plans for the next day, when she put her arms around me and we suddenly started to kiss. It was impulsive, like we were following a script, a pre-written set of instructions, and I *knew* then that we were about to sleep together. Her face was so loving and beautiful and my heart was pounding like mad as we continued to kiss wildly and fell back onto the sofa, struggling out of our clothes so that I could feel her soft warm flesh around me. We made love on that same sofa where I had spent so many lonely nights in June—and at that climatic moment, when it really felt as though we were joined into one, and all I wanted to do was to cry out how much in love I was with all the intensity of feeling that I could muster, at that moment it was such blinding ecstasy that it became somehow wonderfully agonising, and we seemed to exist on a higher plane where every emotion was at an impossible extreme. And after a few minutes, when we had calmed down and were just lying there holding each other, it was difficult to understand exactly what had happened; it was kind of a shock—the type of shock that makes you want to cry and yet feel happy at the same time.

That night we both slept in her bed, and although it was lovely to feel her beside me I did not sleep very well. I could not stop thinking about her Internet stripping. It mattered more now; the hurt pierced me more deeply than I had thought possible. Somehow it had become harder than ever to talk about. And then the thought struck me that perhaps I should ask her to marry me, to go out and buy an engagement ring. We would be together then, no matter what stood in the way. Perhaps if we were engaged then she would stop, perhaps I could find a job at university and make extra money for us that way.

I still could not really believe what had just happened. A car rumbled down the road. I knew that I would always love her now, that I could never love another woman. Eventually I fell asleep and sometime during the night it began to rain.

Chapter Fourteen

The furniture store, on a dull Saturday afternoon, was a strangely comforting place to be. Sofas, polished tables and wooden beds were oddly attractive and almost exciting in their unused state, waiting for a home to go to where they would be absorbed, day by day, into the stretch of life. Watching Eva speak with a couple of customers, I wondered how long some of the chairs for sale would be in use for, which of them bought that day would remain for years in a family home; children, grandchildren, infinite mealtimes seated around on the same few chairs, lives changing and aging but the furniture surviving it all.

It was quite a small store, and besides Eva there was only one other person working there, a woman of about thirty-five years who was very friendly but could not speak English. She had no problem with me being there, so while Eva worked her shift, from two o'clock until six, I walked around the shop, examining the different items for sale, noting the clean, sweet air, and thinking about the past days.

When we awoke on Friday morning, we had not mentioned the previous evening's lovemaking. I suppose that we did not act much differently than usual, as though there were no need to talk about it, though I felt it would only be polite to make some comment.

'I enjoyed last night,' I said at breakfast, staring down into my cereal bowl.

'Yes, me too.'

We hadn't mentioned it again, though it was very much with us during the day. That was the way with these physical changes in a relationship, I thought. They weren't things that were obvious to the outsider, more of a feeling between the two of us, invisible yet very strong.

I wondered when we would sleep together again. I wanted to, it was exciting and frightening to think about, and I wanted to as soon as possible. God, she was wonderful; I needed to feel that warm skin again, to burn with the extremity of our love. And yet that great horror was still nearby, the thought of her as a stripper, of men paying to see her perform, show of her body for them to drool over, an invasion of our happiness. It was just too much for me to deal with, to think coherently about, as though I could not hold the joy and anguish in my mind at the same time. Nothing else was important anymore, not even the man at Munich station. Perhaps, I thought, the jealously that had cut me so often would be reduced in the future, now that we had become so close. If only she hadn't told me about her Internet job, perhaps everything would be wonderful—but no, there was no point in wishing for ignorance.

Walking to the shop-front, I looked out across the road. At four o'clock the afternoon was very quiet, and there were few people strolling past. Eva had told me that the busiest days were when it rained, when parents would bring their children and spend an hour examining new furniture as a way of passing a restless Saturday. On the other side of the street there were more shops, one of which appeared to be a small restaurant which was closed. Despite having two more hours with nothing to do, I thought that it was better to be inside than outdoors. There was something depressing, almost menacing, in the grey pavement and the cloud-covered sky.

I turned back and saw Eva walking towards me, between rows of sofas. Suddenly, I experienced a peculiar sensation, a kind of strong magnetic pull towards her. The shape of her face and her hair seemed to draw me towards her without thinking.

'I get a break now for ten minutes or so,' she said as we met. 'Would you like a drink?'

'Yes, please.' I realised that, as far as I could see, there were only two customers left in the shop. We sat at a little plastic table in the far corner, near a collection of wardrobes, and drank a cup of coffee each.

'It's quieter than normal today,' Eva remarked, looking back towards the front door.'

'I thought it must be, hardly anyone's come in so far.'

'I wish it would be like this every Saturday.' She ran a finger along the tabletop.

'What do you think we should do tomorrow?' I asked.

'I was thinking that we should go on a trip somewhere, for a day out.'

'That's a good idea. Whereabouts should we go?'

'There are lots of interesting places around here, not too far on a train. We'll see what the weather's like.'

Footsteps approached, and a man swung into view around the corner. He was about forty, and very tall, whistling loudly a tune that I half-recognised.

Though the night was made for loving,
And the day returns too soon,
Yet we'll no more go a-roving
By the light of the moon.

He smiled at us and went into one of the office rooms at the back.

'He works here,' Eva said, grinning.

'I think you have more employees than customers.' Looking across at her smile, I wondered how I would manage to cope when we were apart again. It would probably be harder now, I thought. It would be painful just to wake without her in the mornings.

'Are you bored?' she asked.

'It's not too bad, hanging around the shop.' I had been worried at first that a customer might mistake me for an assistant and ask me a question, but this seemed unlikely.

'Next week this time you'll be at home, won't you?' she asked, intercepting my thoughts.

'Yes, I suppose I will. I'll probably get home about mid-day on Saturday.' I drained the remains of my cup. 'It'll be sad, to think of you working here again when I'm so far away.'

A few minutes later, Eva had to continue her shift, and I went back to strolling around the shop. Now though, I thought only of one issue. For the last two days I had been pondering whether Eva and I should be engaged, and the more I thought about it the more of a possibility it seemed. Perhaps, when she realised how serious I was, she would give up her job as a stripper. Certainly it would mean that we could talk about the issue. More than that though, if we were engaged it would make everything so much easier; being apart would not be quite as painful, because we would have a lifetime together to look forward to. My heart beat faster as I thought about it. I could imagine telling my friends at university when the new semester began.

'How was your time in Germany?' Dan would ask. 'Jason tells me that you went twice in the end.'

'That's right,' I would reply, unable to stop smiling.

'So,' he would continue, 'how was your girl?'

'Well, actually,' I would leave a slight pause, 'actually, we're engaged now.'

'Engaged? Blimey, congratulations!' I would tell my friends as soon as I met them, and then, sometime a few days later, a friend who I had not previously seen, would come up to me and say with a grin, 'I heard some terrible news about you. Is it true that you're engaged?'

And I would say, 'I'm afraid so. Isn't it awful?'

And we would both laugh, and the friend would ask, 'So, when's the big day going to be?'

'We don't have an exact date yet,' I would explain, 'but probably sometime next summer.'

Just thinking about it made me glow inside. Perhaps, of course, it would be better to wait for two years, by which time I would have finished my degree. She didn't even know when her degree would be completed. Everything about her life seemed so stale, years wasting away as she aged — together we would help each other, move away from her family restrictions and gain a purpose.

It was all possible, I thought. If I asked her, surely she would say yes, especially after all that had happened in the last few days. And there was a jewellery shop just fifteen minutes' walk from her flat. Best to ask her before buying a ring, for one thing I wasn't exactly sure what size was required. Perhaps I would ask her on Tuesday or Wednesday, in the morning so I would not feel nervous all day. Then we would walk together to the jewellery shop to buy the ring.

Lost in my thoughts, I found that the hours passed very quickly and soon it was six o'clock and time to leave.

'The weather is supposed to be good tomorrow,' Eva said as we stepped onto the street. 'In the morning we can decide which town to visit.'

'I'll have to leave it up to you,' I said. 'You're the expert on this region.'

'Not really, I'm afraid.'

'Well, you know it better than I do.' Now that we were together, I realised how nerve-wracking it would be to even talk about engagement. I tried to imagine asking her, and I knew that it would take a lot of courage.

'We should phone Jens at some point as well,' she continued.

'Yes, we must meet him again before I leave.'

The day was quite chilly, and even with a coat on I was a little cold. We walked quickly, past a garage and rows of small shops and houses. As we approached the bus stop, which lay around the corner of a building, there was a lot of shouting from somewhere in front of us. It sounded as though a dangerous argument were going on, and I was worried that the people who were shouting might be waiting at the bus stop, in which case we would have to wait with them. As we turned the corner though, there was no sign of any trouble and the noise stopped.

The bus journey back home was slow, but quite pleasant. We reached the main bus station and changed to the route that would drop us near Eva's flat, and this took us past the jewellery shop. It was closed as we trundled by, but I felt a thrill of excitement, of dreams that could be fulfilled. Yet it was an excitement mixed with fear, of looming crisis and almost pleasurable pain, of surrendering to what might be a foolish desire. The dream and the nightmare were no longer separate.

On the next day we went to one of the big, beautiful medieval towns of the region, though to begin with I would have preferred to have stayed in bed. We made love again that morning, this time in Eva's bed, not long after waking up. And this time, a few minutes after we had finished, I felt so depressed for a while that I couldn't believe it was real. It seemed that everything was turning grey and lonely.

'What's the matter?' Eva asked.

'Nothing.'

'You look like you're crying.'

'No, no I'm not. I was just thinking.'

'Thinking about what?'

'Just about things. About you, and us.'

'What things?'

'Oh, just things, it doesn't matter.' I ran my fingers through her hair. She reached across and picked up the alarm clock.

'We can stay in bed for another ten minutes,' she decided, 'and then we'll have to get a move on.'

'Where are we going?'

'I'll show you on a map in a while.'

I felt a lot better then, and wished that we didn't have to get up at all. It was so lovely just to be able to sit there and hold each other that I would have liked to have stayed in bed all day. We set out on time though, and by ten o'clock were on a train heading south on the half-hour journey. It was a hot day and the brown fields that we passed were strong and full of life, a kind of beauty in the changing season.

'Eva,' I said after a while, 'when are we going to see each other next? After I go home, I mean.'

'I don't know.' She didn't look at me.

'I mean, do you think that we should meet again before Christmas?'

'My next holiday is not until Christmas.'

'No, nor is mine. Still, I could take a few days off from uni to visit you. What do you think?'

'I don't know.' She looked uncomfortable.

'Well, would you like to meet again before Christmas?'

She did not answer, but peered intently out of the window.

'Would you?' I asked.

'Yes, of course.'

'That's good.'

A distant tractor worked a far-off field. Gazing at the view I wondered whether it would be possible for us to meet again before Christmas. Otherwise it would be a three-month wait until the next holiday.

'The first time I went to this town was on a school trip,' Eva said.

'How old were you then?'

'About eleven, I think.'

About eleven. I would have been two at the time. I want to ask her to marry me, but she'll be almost middle-aged in ten years' time, but we're so much in love.

'Have you been back since?' I asked.

'Once or twice.'

It was strange to know that she had memories of days before I was born, that she could think back and remember her early childhood of twenty years ago, yet for me these times did not exist, had never existed. I continued to watch the landscape rush past. Had these fields changed at all in twenty, thirty years? Would they ever change? Generations of rail passengers could travel this line and see just about the same sights, and perhaps it would stir in them similar feelings, as though we were all somehow linked through time.

When we arrived in the town I was more impressed than I had expected to be. It was picturesque without feeling lost in the past—rows of old, wood-beamed houses flanked ancient streets, and all around were wonderful views down from the hill on which it was built and across the glowing countryside. We set out amid hundreds of other tourists, many of whom were heading towards the shops at the town centre, and spent a pleasant couple of hours in the sun, exploring the history around us, feeling almost a part of it.

'I think I remember this from when I came before,' Eva said as we stood beneath a medieval tower around midday.

'What is it?'

'Just an old tower, I think.'

'Shall we take a look?' I walked to the entrance expecting to see a ticket booth, but the stone doorway was deserted so we assumed it was free to enter.

Inside, there were two or three other tourists on the single floor that was open. There was a very damp, unpleasant smell, and I felt that it was not a happy place.

'I remember now,' Eva was saying. 'I'm sure that this tower had something to do with the Thirty Years' War.'

'What exactly?'

'Well, that's the problem, I can't remember. It was probably something I heard when I was on the school trip.'

Standing in the cold tower, I thought about the Thirty Years' War, about the great religious struggles that tore Europe apart at the end of the sixteenth and first half of the seventeenth centuries. It was unsettling to think of the old nations crumbling, changing and merging, of old orders collapsing, of men and women living in fear because of their beliefs. The day seemed to grow darker, and I thought again of the figure that had stood in front of me by the town hall in Munich, as though that same figure had stood here four hundred years ago and witnessed the suffering that boiled around him; and somehow I also saw Eva, here on a school trip seventeen years ago, long, long before she ever knew I existed.

'Are you feeling hungry yet?' she asked, turning from the window.

'I am rather. How about you?'

'Yes, very hungry. Let's find somewhere to eat.'

We stepped back into the sunlight and walked towards the town centre until we found a small kebab shop. It was tiny inside, just three tables for customers, so I assumed that it was mainly a takeaway. Eva ordered us a kebab each and we sat on the green, plastic chairs to eat, watching the crowds go past in the street.

'I can't believe how cheap these were,' I said, 'only five marks. That's half of what you would pay in England.'

'I know; most food is cheap here.'

'Do you remember Jason, from university?' I asked, smiling.

'Vaguely, yes.'

'He would love kebabs this cheap.'

'Perhaps he should come here one day.'

'Yes, he probably should.' I paused for a moment. 'Can you hear music somewhere?'

'No,' she said, listening, 'no, I can't here any music.'

'I'm probably imagining it.' It was strange, but I could distinctly hear the soft notes of a piano, playing a slow melody; yet it did not seem to be real, coming more from within my mind that the world outside.

'My mother would hate this kind of food,' Eva grinned, rolling a long strand of doner meat around her fork.

'Are we going to see your mother again this week?' I asked.

'I'm not sure. We might.'

A group of Japanese tourists passed by the window. I no longer heard the music, and instead I thought about Eva's mother and wondered what she thought of me. I wondered whether she would be happy if we were engaged.

'I'm not sure that I can finish this,' I said, regarding the still sizeable remains of my kebab, the brown-white bread wrapped around a few strands of meat.

'Well, we can leave when you want to.' Eva had already abandoned the rest of her food, so we smiled goodbye to the man behind the counter and went back out to the street.

The rest of the afternoon was lovely. We strolled through a park at the edge of the town, and it was like the middle of summer, happy family groups with children playing on the swings and parents lazing on a bench beneath the sun, and it seemed that the day had removed all our troubles, so that just for a little we could walk together without worry, without fear for the future. At one point we found ourselves on a high ridge, looking down over a breathtaking view of colourful fields stretching out to where small hills rose up in the distance, crossed by tiny roads and the shimmering haze of life, as though all nature stood before us, the known and the unknown glimpsed for an instant in reality. We stood, holding hands and gazing into the valley, and it seemed that we were closer then than ever before, that our minds and souls were fused together in a union that would never end. Then a big woman asked us to move so she could take a photo and the spell was broken, but it was a special moment nonetheless.

In the early evening we returned to the station to catch the train home. There was a twenty-minute wait, so we sat on one of the long benches beside the rather grimy walls, and watched the few people move about us and the occasional train pass though. There was a slightly uncomfortable feeling to the platform, and I wished that we did not have to wait at all.

'Did you enjoy coming here for your school trip?' I asked.

'I can't really remember. I suppose so; anything's better than being in school.'

'That's true. I wonder when we'll come here next.'

'Perhaps at Christmas.' She closed her eyes.

I could not remove the thought of the next Friday's departure from my mind. It seemed so cruel that I had to leave. And would we ever come here again? I looked at Eva and wondered whether we should be engaged. Surely it was my one hope, I could not imagine surviving an entire university term without her unless we had made that special commitment which would give me the security that I needed. I could never love another woman, I thought; it just wouldn't work after being with Eva. I would never be able to fully enjoy sleeping with another girl, it might be good but it would never be *as* good, and I would be forever looking back to these days when there was still a chance of making things work between us. Yes, getting engaged was the only answer — and yet, of course, it wasn't that simple. I could not see the future, could not know what a life with Eva would really be like, despite all that I already knew about her.

It was growing colder, and we were both glad when the train arrived to sweep us through the evening and home.

Chapter Fifteen

By Wednesday morning, as the bus trawled across the morning city, I could feel a climax approaching. Monday and Tuesday had flashed past as we explored markets and fairs and bier gartens, my mind confused and still unwilling to focus. It was love that drew us through the cool September afternoons, yet always there was the terror of the truth that I could not forget. There were just three days left, and I knew that I would have to make a decision soon; in fact I already had a plan. Eva and I had decided to spend the morning visiting the city museum, after which I had arranged to visit Jens for a few hours. The thought had occurred to me that, if I wanted to talk seriously with Eva about our being engaged, then perhaps the best time to do this would be upon my return from Jens, sometime in the early evening.

My heart beat fast as I wondered whether or not I would ask her. The bus was very busy, and at every stop at least half a dozen people left and another half dozen boarded. We pulled through small roads and further towards the medieval city centre, a babble of voices and movement, the plastic floor grey and speckled with mud.

'When did you last go to the museum?' I asked.

'It must have been sometime last year,' Eva replied, turning her gaze from the window. 'I went there with the university.'

'How long do you think it'll take us to look around?'

'Oh, a few hours. What time did you say you would meet Jens?'

'About one o'clock. I'm going to take the bus to his village.'

'That's brave of you.'

Actually, I was beginning to regret my decision. When I had spoken to Jens that morning and told him that I would arrive at his house by bus, it had surprised me considerably. It had been a heat-of-the-moment decision, as I didn't want to put him to too much trouble by having to pick me up, but now the journey alone seemed a lot more difficult.

We arrived at the museum, located in an imposing, grey building of stern architecture, and bought the tickets. The whole city centre was rather frightening, belonging so obviously to a different age that the men and women who walked its streets seemed lost and out of place, and I was glad to enter the museum which, despite being old, had its history under control.

We spent the morning examining the various displays, relics of a dark past holding their secrets deep within them. Eva was in a cheerful mood; we held hands most of the way around, and I felt very happy and proud to be with her, especially when somebody glanced at us and noticed us together. I wondered whether she was proud to be with me as well.

The section which moved me the most deeply was a room dedicated to the Holy Roman Empire, that great union centred on Germany throughout the Middle Ages and up until early-modern times. The empire was an assembly of states, city-states and territories, ruled by their own kings, princes, counts and clerics. The emperor himself was chosen by a group of seven electors; three bishops and four laymen. What struck me most strongly was that, in later years, the emperor had usually been crowned at Frankfurt. Frankfurt, that confusing city where I had met Eva three months before, where I had returned to alone again upon our parting. It did not seem possible that coronations had taken place there. It made me feel dizzy to think of it—the emperor-elect travelling to Frankfurt in all his glory to lead the ancient empire, and myself, hundreds of years later, standing in the same city, following my dreams on the ruins of the old order. And, standing in that dull room, I wondered how far we really were from those times. It seemed that, beyond the museum, the dark roads were those of the ancient empire, that the emperor himself paced wearily along the old German streets, past men and women of bygone days whose lives' desires had rotted with them, leaving only the odd scar on history. It wasn't a pleasant feeling, and I held Eva's hand a little more tightly until we passed on.

Eventually, having toured most of the building, we found ourselves in a little restaurant and decided to have a cup of coffee before leaving. It was a quiet room with just two other tables occupied, and the coffee was served in a large pot so there was more than one cup each. I watched Eva tear open a little packet of sugar and stir it into her drink.

'At Christmas,' I said, 'will you visit me in England?'

'I don't know,' she seemed annoyed that I had raised the subject. 'It depends how my mother is.'

'Just it would mean a lot to me if you could visit me at home.'

'We'll have to see later on. There's no point in arranging anything yet.'

'I guess not.' I wished that we could have our next meeting planned, in fact I wished that we had our next two or three meetings planned, so that I wouldn't have to worry about them.

Two parents and two small children entered the room and sat at the next table. I sipped my coffee and wondered vaguely what they thought of us.

'When you take the bus to Jens,' Eva said, 'you'll have to go from here to the university town, and then change buses and take one for his village.'

'Right. Do you know the bus number that I'll need?'

'No, but it should have the stops displayed at the front.'

'I'm sure it'll be fine.' Changing buses, that might be difficult. Again, I wished that I had accepted a lift from Jens.

'We had coffee here when I came with the university,' Eva said, fiddling with a sugar packet.

'Yes, it's very nice in here.' Always it made me feel sad to think of her doing things without me. I thought again of our possible engagement. 'Eva, what do you see for your future?'

'How do you mean?'

'I mean, what do you think you'll be doing in one year, or two years?'

'I don't know, probably the same as always.'

There was no point in asking subtle questions. I knew that the only way to solve the issue was to ask her directly. *Perhaps tonight then.*

We sat drinking our coffee, and it was so peaceful and relaxing that I could have happily ordered another cup. It was almost half past twelve though, so we left the museum and walked to the bus stop.

'You'll be all right on this journey then, won't you?' Eva asked.

'Yes, of course. What are you going to do this afternoon?'

'Just some work probably. I have essays to write for next semester.'

'That's harsh. I'll be back at about five o'clock, so we can do something this evening if you want.'

'I think this is your bus now,' she put her hand on my arm and pushed me towards the small queue. I remembered my mother doing something similar many years before.

'I look forward to seeing you tonight then,' I said.

'Yes, see you then.'

I climbed onto the bus with the others, and she waved goodbye from the pavement. We pulled away, and I felt such a tug of the heart at leaving her standing there that I wondered how we would ever cope with being separated again. It felt as though we were both a part of each other, that I could not properly exist without her; but it was a wonderful feeling as well as a sad one.

And as we rolled though the busy, foreign streets, a sweeping freedom began to lift my spirit. It was so strange to be on my own—an unknown man took the seat next to me as rows of shops drifted past—and it was like growing up. I was no longer an alien, no longer afraid of being different. It was my city now as much as anybody's. I thought of a bird taking flight across the sea, of trials overcome. For a while there was no fear.

I enjoyed the journey, and when we arrived at the university town I had no difficulty in finding the right bus for the trip to Jens's village. I suppose it was during the second part of the trip, the ten minutes or so through countryside, that I made the decision to talk with Eva that night about being engaged. There was no sudden resolution on my part, rather I gradually realised that it was my only choice. Through the window I could see grassland and meadows, cattle grazing in large fields under the weak sun. The year was turning to autumn with such beauty, and I knew that I wanted to be with Eva forever. No matter what problems faced us, our love was surely worth every sacrifice.

I made the short walk from the bus stop to Jens's house feeling happy and excited. Having decided to act that evening gave a thrilling aspect to the whole day, a kind of exhilarating relief that the months of insecurity would come to an end.

'Good afternoon,' Jens greeted me, opening the door.

'Hello, how are you?'

'Fine, really.' He led the way inside and through to the kitchen. 'I was just about to eat. Would you like anything?'

'Yes, please, I'm starving.' A part of me wished that Jens knew all that had happened since we had last met. His house felt so homely, it was as though we were related.

'My parents are out, I'm afraid,' he said, setting out cold meat and bread on the table.

'That's a shame, I would have liked to have seen them again.'

'You do not think that you'll return here then, before you leave?'

'Well, I'm going back on Friday, so I don't have much time.' I reached for some bread. 'I would like to visit more often, but of course I want to spend as much time as possible with Eva.'

'Yes, of course.'

'One day we should go on a holiday somewhere together, perhaps in England.'

'I would like to visit England again.' He took a slice of cold ham from its packet. 'It would be good to see some of the other guys from university as well.'

'Hell, perhaps we could all meet up sometime,' I said, but it was a little sad because I knew that really we never would.

'One day in England,' Jens said, looking at his watch. 'What time do you want to return?'

'I told Eva that I'd be home for five.' It was lovely, really; it sounded as though we were married already.

'So you've enjoyed your visits to the Continent this summer?' Jens asked.

'Yes, very much so.'

'And how have you enjoyed being with Eva?'

'Well, I mean, it's been great, obviously. I'm hoping that I can convince her to come to England for Christmas.'

'That would be nice.'

'She doesn't seem to be too keen though. She's worried that she may have to look after her mother.'

'Ah.'

'Actually, if you see her around then try to convince her to stay with me at Christmas. It'd be great to show her my home.'

'Maybe if I see her I'll try.' He took a bite of his sandwich.

'Do you ever wish —'

'Ever wish what?'

'Do you ever wish that you could go back, right back in time and start everything again?'

'Everybody wishes that sometimes.'

'Yes, I guess so.'

'Why? Is that what you want now?'

'No.' I thought for a moment. 'No, I don't think it is, not at the moment.'

That afternoon we went for a walk around the village, the late sun glimmering its faded warmth on the old homes. As time passed I began to feel more and more anxious about the evening's talk with Eva. I tried to plan what to say, but it was no good. The whole day, in fact the whole summer, was focusing down onto a few moments. As we walked, it felt as though Jens were my comrade in war, and I was preparing to go off and fight the great battle, the great battle that I had to fight alone. And it was odd, but I felt that asking Eva to marry me would not be done simply for the two of us. It would be done for Jens, for Dan and Jason, for everybody whom I knew, somehow allowing me to be their equal, to have achieved something in the world that was worthy of respect.

At four-thirty Jens offered to give me a lift home, and we walked out to the driveway. It was quite sad, leaving his house for what could be the last time in a long while, but my mind was on other matters.

'What are you planning to do tonight?' he asked, reversing out onto the road.

'I'm not sure,' I lied, nerves stabbing me. It would be wonderful to tell Jens, I thought. Surely Eva would say yes. We would phone Jens tomorrow and tell him, and he would probably joke about how it had been obvious that there was something on my mind, and he was relieved that it wasn't anything more serious.

The journey back to the city felt like a symbolic trip, a spiritual return to Eva. I was so nervous that it brought a strange sense of calm, oddly enjoyable. Our route actually took us past the jewellery shop and, as we were obliged to wait at traffic lights just opposite it, I had the chance to look inside, and noticed that it was still open.

'I wonder when that place closes,' I said.

'That shop stays open until quite late, perhaps even eight o'clock,' Jens replied, glancing across. 'Why, are you thinking of buying something for Eva?'

'I might.' We may even be able to buy a ring that night, I thought. Originally I had planned to ask her in the morning so we had all day, but if the place was open late then we might as well go at once. Well, it didn't really matter, we had another two days, just it was an option if we felt like it. Somehow, I

thought, the actual act of buying a ring would make it all official.

We turned into another familiar road, and I was so tense
that I could hardly speak. *Surely just a couple of minutes now till
you arrive, you may have actually asked her in ten minutes' time.* A
few young boys slouched along the pavement; inside a restaurant I could see several happy families drinking wine. *These are
the moments you'll remember forever; God, it's too much, what are
you going to say? How are you going to ask her?* I could hear
music in my head again, not slow this time, but a kind of dis-
cord, violinists plucking random strings. I thought of those terrible, jealousy-ridden visits to nightclubs, the sort that I could
perhaps banish forever with the certainty of our commitment.
*You'll be grown-up at last, no more games. You'll be above all the
fear, all the lost souls who walk these streets.* Into Eva's road now,
we pulled up alongside her flat and I felt as though my soul
were tearing itself apart as Jens lifted the handbrake.

'Well,' I said, climbing out onto the pavement which
seemed to move beneath my feet, 'I don't know whether we
shall meet again this year, but I might see you at Christmas.'

'Yes, it's certainly been good to see you again.' He sat
with the engine running.

'Say hello to your parents for me, then; and I look forward to seeing you all again soon.'

'Yes, goodbye for now.'

'Bye.' I watched him pull away, and then turned toward
the flat. As I approached the front door, it was opened by a
woman who smiled at me before stepping outside and hurrying down the path. I entered, closed the door, and began to
mount the stairs, my heart pounding so hard that it was actually difficult to climb them. Arriving at Eva's door, I knocked
without hesitating.

'Hello,' she said, stepping aside to let me enter. 'How was
Jens?'

'He's very well, but I'd rather be with you.' I suddenly
felt incredibly awkward, as though whatever I said were going
to be wrong. The smell of the flat filled my mind.

'It's been a quiet afternoon here.' She walked through to the kitchen. I followed her, wishing that I'd planned what to say more carefully.

'Eva, there's something I want to ask you.'

'Yes?' She looked straight into my eyes.

'I've been thinking for a while about us, and—' I paused for an instant, just finding the strength to ask the question, but she interrupted.

'By the way, I have to go out in a minute.'

'We have to talk first.'

'Actually I have to go in about five minutes.'

'Where are you going?' Suddenly I was angry, tense and angry. These should have been our special moments, if only she would listen.

'I have to go to my job.' She rested her hands on the table, and there was guilt in her eyes.

'What job?'

'The Internet thing.'

'No.' It wasn't possible, surely not. I had painted it out of existence. 'No, don't go there.'

'I have to. They phoned and said that they needed me tonight, unexpectedly. I get paid more though, because it's unexpected.'

'So, you're going to go and be a stripper tonight?' I could feel tears in my eyes.

'Yes, I have to.'

'I see.' I was not angry anymore; I was not even nervous. In a moment all the desire, all the lust had vanished. She was just a child now, a sad, misguided child whom I could not save. A child for whom I would give anything to make happy, for whom I would destroy my own life if only it would help her a little; but I knew that it was no good.

'I'm sorry to have to rush out,' she said, 'I'm just glad that you arrived back before I had to leave.'

'Yes, it's lucky.'

'I'll be back at about ten. Will you still be awake then?'

'Yeah, yeah, I'll still be awake.'

'You can read a book or something. And I'll leave you my spare keys in case you want to go out. You'll be all right, won't you?'

'Yeah, I'll be all right.'

And when she had gone, I went through to the living room and slumped down on the sofa and lay there for an hour, unable to move. It was my own fault, I thought; nothing had really changed that evening. I had always known that this might happen. It was impossible to ignore; I may be able to put it out of mind for a while, but it would always return in the end. A few shouts echoed from the street, but I didn't seem to be in the room at all, not a part of reality, my soul too empty to be among life.

After an hour passed, though, I began to wonder if there was still hope, whether I had given up too easily. After all, I had never actually asked her to marry me, and were we engaged then perhaps she would give up her stripping, perhaps it could still save her. Checking the time I realised that the jewellery shop was probably still open. I was fairly sure of the ring size that I needed, and a little excitement began to stir again. I could go out right away and buy her a ring, then when she returned in the evening I could present it too her, say how much I loved her and how much her stripping was hurting me, and maybe everything would be sorted out.

Anyway, I left the flat, went out onto the silent road, and stood for a while wondering whether to walk to the shop. The sky was growing dull and the air stank of exhaust fumes. From far away I could hear music cutting across the hollow city. It wasn't any good; I simply could not bring myself to buy Eva an engagement ring while she was stripping in a studio for men in America. I had always known it really. Yet even after I had made the decision I stood for a long time looking at the road and the sky.

Chapter Sixteen

On Friday morning, at about ten o'clock, it began to rain. Standing at the sitting-room window I watched the haze descend across the opposite flats, the occasional big drop splattering against the glass by my face. Soon the paving stones of the garden below had turned from grey to black beneath the torrent; it was the final collapse of the summer, the dream dissolved and swept away.

'What time shall we eat?' Eva asked, standing behind me.

'About twelve?' I felt numb and nervous with the long journey ahead of me. We had decided that I would catch the six o'clock train to Munich, and Eva would be able to accompany me only as far as the city station because of her furniture store job the next day.

Every part of me felt empty. Watching a man with an umbrella rush across the garden, I knew that the challenge we had set ourselves had failed, that it was not enough just to love somebody and imagine that this would overcome all problems. Yet I was no longer an alien; standing at the window I surveyed a few blocks of a city that was almost home, though by tomorrow I would be far away, perhaps never to return. Perhaps never? Didn't we both know, both sense in a way that neither of us would admit, that something was finished? Ever since Wednesday night that invisible feeling between us had been different, as though something that we had known all along had finally become apparent.

'I think we should have a pizza for dinner, what do you think?' Eva asked.

'That'd be great. Do we have any?' I walked through to join her in the kitchen.

'Yes, there's one in the freezer.' She pulled a ready-made pizza from between several other boxes, a few flakes of ice falling to the floor. Watching her, a great part of me wished that we could go on living together for the rest of our lives. It still felt like we were married.

There was a knock at the front door, and Eva went to answer it.

'My mother's here,' she called a few moments later.

'Really?' I was amazed. Eva had said that her mother hardly ever left her flat these days, and it made me wonder how great the danger of her dropping in had been during my first, unofficial, visit. For her to have braved the rain was quite astonishing.

Eva made coffee and we all went through to the sitting room.

'My mother took a taxi here,' she whispered to me as we sat on the sofa while the old woman examined the mantelpiece. 'She wanted to see you again before you left.'

'That's really nice of her.' I felt a flush of happiness that I was being accepted, though it all seemed rather hollow. I had worried about Eva's mother once, worried about the people around us who might have done us damage, but in the end it was only ourselves that really mattered.

'She wants to know when you will visit again,' Eva told me as her mother sat in the armchair, looking slightly awkward as though she were not entirely comfortable in my presence.

'Soon,' I said. 'Perhaps at Christmas, but maybe Eva will visit me then in England.' Her mother didn't understand what I said, of course, and I think that when Eva translated she missed out the last bit.

The sad thing about us all sitting there was that it was a glimpse of something that could have been, if only the situation was different: Eva and I, together, being visited by her family, being proud to have a home where we could receive guests and then return to our normal day. Still, it was pleasant to meet Eva's mother again, even though we could hardly communicate. We sat for half an hour and talked as best we could, though none of us managed to really relax. Sometimes I looked into the old woman's eyes and wondered what she meant by the half-fearful glances she gave her daughter from the corners of her eyes. I was very aware of the sofa beneath me, as though it were about to swallow me up, an unsettling feeling that I did not understand. The whole visit was quite awkward, but when the old woman departed I felt quite sorry to see her go, wondering whether I had made a good impression for all my lack of linguistic talent.

'Well, that was a surprise,' Eva said as she closed the door.

'It certainly was.'

'That's the first time she's been here for almost a year.'

'Nice of her to come and see me.' I picked up the pizza box and glanced at the heating instructions. It was still strange to see foreign words.

'Well, we'd better cook this,' Eva said, taking the box from me.

'I love your voice,' I said.

'Pardon?'

'I love your accent, the way you speak.'

'Oh I don't think I'm so good at pronouncing English words.' She seemed flustered.

'Yes you are, you speak beautifully, much nicer than with a normal English accent.'

'We'd better get on and cook this pizza,' she said.

I would have liked to have gone out after we had eaten, just for a walk to remove the miserable tension that came from staying inside too long, but the rain continued and it hardly seemed worth getting soaked. Eventually we switched on the television and sat half-watching, half-thinking. I put my arms around Eva and held her very close, and the afternoon drifted along while we talked and laughed, and we did not discuss the future very much.

The clock above the mantelpiece continued to count away our time, the second hand slipping around, unceasingly declaring moments forever past. I wondered what Eva was thinking about. She was so warm, and after all, whenever I held her in my arms it felt as though a little of our souls were mingling together, as though our spirits were merging and becoming one. But what was left for the future? Voices, faded now but still clear, whispered at the edges of my mind. *You'll never find anyone like her again, anyone who's so perfect for you, who's even the right age. You'll never be able to fall in love again, to sleep with a woman who's everything you want.* It was a childish voice, repeating over and over again, and I did not challenge it. I did not even understand my feelings — that afternoon there was no great physical desire, just a need to be very close, to protect, to comfort as though there were some hope remaining. Yet beyond the tiny flat there was a whole world that was dividing us, a world in which we were doomed to live our separate lives; a maddening whirl of music and sorrow.

> *When I am dead, my dearest,*
> *Sing no sad songs for me;*
> *Plant thou no roses at my head,*
> *Nor shady cypress tree*

My eyes flickered across the few ornaments on the mantelpiece, around the room which Eva would continue to use every day when I was gone. I wanted time to hurry away so that the pain of the journey would be over, but at the same moment I wanted our final few hours to last forever.

'Eva,' I said eventually, 'you do love me, don't you?'

'What?'

'Do you love me?'

'Yes, yes.'

'Good, yes, I know it really,' there were tears in my eyes but I continued, 'it's just nice to hear you say it sometimes.'

'So,' she said after a pause, 'when are we going to meet next?'

'At Christmas, I suppose.'

'Yes.'

'Unless you want to meet earlier.' I took hold of her hand.
'How?'

'Well, we could plan something, but it wouldn't be easy.'

'No, it wouldn't be easy.'

'Christmas is not too far away.' I felt that I should say
more, but couldn't find the right words.

'Do you remember,' she said at last, 'that pub we used to
go to at university in England, the one with the darts players,
do you remember it?'

'Yes, I remember. That was our favourite pub.' My heart
was suddenly heavy as I thought of a dark student bar with
four or five people always clustered around the darts board,
Eva and I sitting on the old chairs, half watching the game, so
excited just to be with each other. 'Perhaps we'll go back there
one day,' I said.

'Perhaps we will.'

A gust of wind tossed the rain against the window, and
the clock hands slid on.

At five o'clock, after a brief meal which I didn't feel like eating, we left the flat to head to the train station. This involved a
trip across the underground, for which the nearest station was
fifteen minutes' walk away.

'Well, I guess I've got everything,' I said, lifting my suitcase and taking a last glance around the room. The rain still
hammered down outside and everything was gloomy; the
journey home was a trip with no reward at the end of it, the
payment after the benefit.

'We'd better go then.' Eva led the way into the corridor
and locked the door. We went down in the lift and out of the
main door into the wet street. Everything smelt of rain and
damp buildings; and, glancing around, it pulled at my heart to
think that the road would probably remain unchanged for
twenty or thirty years' time, to think that were I to walk there
again after the decades had aged us then I would see the same
sights, catch the same smells, even with Eva long gone.

We passed through a few streets, hugging as close to the buildings as possible, but soon we were both drenched. After five minutes we turned out into a deserted park and hurried along the path which cut across it. The air was heavy, rustling from the wet grass like a mist of memories. I felt Eva very close beside me, as though she had always been there, as though she were always going to be there.

'Do you remember that man we met at the Munich station?' she asked, sounding quite out of breath.

'Yes, I remember.'

'He said that I should go on the train with him. He was totally crazy.'

'Yes,' I laughed, 'yes, he was.' I felt she was trying to apologise for something.

We hurried on through the soaking city while a car horn blared in the distance. It had all been going on for hundreds of years, I thought, and it will continue for hundreds more. Men and women hurrying in the rain, sitting cosy inside and listening to it lash against their windows, then in the summer walking slowly for the heat, heads confused as they stroll around the estates and the parks and the factories. If I were to return after fifty years then everything would seem much the same as before, yet it would no longer belong to me, for Eva would be old or dead or long since moved away, and the invisible dreams that the ancient streets had once contained would be as lost to me as my own distant youth.

By the time we reached the underground station the bottoms of my trousers were sodden, but it didn't seem to matter much. We descended the wide flight of steps away from the rain and into the subterranean chambers, packed with people and the hiss and roar of trains. It was much busier than I had expected and there was quite a crowd waiting at the platform.

'We just take the first train which goes in this direction,' Eva told me, 'and we need to get off at the fourth stop.'

It was almost frightening, as though we had descended into hell and had found it not so different than the world above. Indeed, as we waited I glanced at the people to my left and, just for a moment, seemed to glimpse that same figure which had stood before me in Munich; the dark coat and imposing stance, but looking more closely I lost sight of it among the rush and it could just have been a trick of the light.

We didn't have to wait long, and soon we were speeding beneath the city, though the darkness gave us little impression of moving at all.

'We should be in plenty of time,' I said, checking my watch.

'Yes, but it's always best to leave early.' Eva interlaced her fingers and peered through the window where there was only blackness. We sat side by side, while on the seats opposite us a young man read a newspaper and a middle-aged woman looked bored. *These people will be here when you've gone. You're going home.* I wished that Eva and I could be alone again, could somehow talk about our problems, but it was too late. After a few minutes we arrived at the main station and almost everybody disembarked with us.

'It looks like your train is already here,' Eva said as we climbed the stairs and arrived at my platform.

'Are you sure? We've still got twenty minutes before it's time to leave.'

'I'll ask somebody.' She approached an official who pointed at the train and nodded. 'Yes,' she said, returning, 'this is the one, it's very early.'

'There's no point in getting on yet, is there?' I asked, my heart beating fast.

'Well, let's both get on, then I'll leave you five minutes before departure time.'

'How about if they check for tickets?'

'My travel card lets me go around this area anyway, so it doesn't matter.'

We climbed onto the train and sat in one of the empty carriages. The seats were red and green, and there was a no smoking sign beside the window.

'So, back to Munich,' I muttered. It was difficult to know what to say.

'Yes, let's hope your flight goes well.'

'We seem to do this a lot, don't we?'

'Do what a lot?'

'Say goodbye.'

'Yes, I suppose we do.'

Two women arrived in the carriage and sat opposite us. I felt annoyed that they had disturbed our last few minutes together; they looked unsympathetic and business-like. I thought of the city again, and then of the tower—that grey mass of steel beyond the still water, seeming to mock us with its mystery. And, as I watched the damp people on the platform dragging suitcases across the gritty tarmac floor, it seemed that all history was spread out haggard before us, that the bleak centuries of human suffering were ever-present, that the great comforts of gas and electricity could not replace the dull spirit of our ancestors which lay deep and lonely in our souls.

Minutes passed and more people arrived in the carriage until it was full. Most of them wore raincoats, which were soaking, and the water ran down onto the floor.

'I'd better go soon,' Eva said.

'Wait another minute.' I took her hand.

'Can you phone me from the airport, just so I know you got there safely?'

'Yes, of course.'

'Do you have any change for the phone?'

'Yes, I've got plenty.' *This shouldn't be happening.*

An elderly man entered the carriage and peered around for a seat. Eve looked at him, and then at me.

'I'd better leave,' she said, smiling.

'Yes, I suppose you had.' I couldn't speak much; my throat was burning.

'Well then, until Christmas,' she kissed me briefly and stood up.

'I'll see you at Christmas.'

'Bye then.' She walked to the end of the carriage and out of the door. All those months of togetherness, that knowledge that we belonged together, and now her going away. The elderly man sat next to me. After a few moments I saw Eva standing on the platform waving, smiling as though nothing were wrong. Looking into her face I thought of walks we had taken though the boiling city streets, of summer music and laughter and whispered words. Then a crowd of ten or twelve young women with suitcases walked in front of her, and when they had passed by she was gone and the grey platform was empty.

I turned and peered out of the opposite window, seeing nothing. I wondered whether the other passengers in the carriage knew that my heart was broken. After a while we began to move, gathering speed and rushing though the city for the final time. Tower blocks jutted upwards against the overcast sky, seeming devoid of life. I didn't want to think about Eva, but I couldn't help it. After all, in the end it hadn't been a case of physical desire as I had thought, sleeping together had not saved us, it had made matters worse in the end. I could see the weeks and months stretching ahead of me, a confusion of fear and anger, tormented by thoughts of her stripping and of our love fading away. We were both to blame, I thought. I had been the one who was always wrecked by jealousy, who was unable to trust, unable to hope. If we were both to be hurt then at least we knew that we shared the blame, that we hurt ourselves as much as each other.

An hour passed, and the rain eased until it eventually stopped altogether. The countryside was still wet though, dark fields and mysterious forests lining our route, seemingly endless as we cut across the land; it was hard to believe that we were heading towards a city, as though all civilisation had been destroyed long ago and there was nothing but the green roll of nature reaching to the distant sea. I was very tired, dreading the long wait at the airport; and listening to the constant rumble of our passage I gradually became aware that I could not feel my feet, indeed it seemed that my legs were completely numb as well. Somehow, I didn't care very much, it was almost pleasant to feel as though I were floating in a different world altogether.

At eight o'clock we stopped at a big station, and most of the people in my carriage left to be replaced by others. A tall woman in her mid-twenties sat opposite me. As we pulled away, a drunken roar echoed along the train, followed immediately by another. My heart quickened a little as I hoped that no drunks would stagger into our carriage, but it was quite a detached fear. The tall woman spoke to me in German.

'Sorry? I'm afraid I don't—'

'You're English, are you?' she asked.

'Yes, that's right.'

'So, I was just saying that it sounds like they're having a good party down there.'

'Were there a lot of drunk people at the station?'

'Yes, they're going into Munich for the night I think, but they're totally drunk already.'

'It makes you wonder what the point is,' I smiled. There were more shouts, but they weren't any closer so I imagined that the drunks were staying in their carriage.

In the distance I could see a castle, rising out of the dull evening. I thought again of the student bar that Eva had mentioned earlier, where there was always a darts game in progress. There had been one night in particular when we had gone to that bar, perhaps our third or fourth date, that I remembered. I had walked across the warm, spring campus to meet Eva at her residence block, thrilled by the thought of the evening ahead, taking pleasure in everything I saw—the daffodils, the football players, the gentle seven o'clock student life. When she opened the door and said hello I felt such a rush of happiness and pride; she was so beautiful at that moment, so innocent and exciting, that the whole of our future, despite its obvious problems, seemed suddenly wonderful. We walked to the bar and sat there for two hours, drinking and laughing, and the world was more full of colour than I had imagined possible. Even the dingy surroundings were special, giving us something to joke about, feeling ourselves drawing closer together. I had told myself then that we would find a way to make it work, that everything would be all right so long as we had love.

And as the train sped onwards with all that dark countryside increasing the distance between us, I ached to go back. Not to return to the city and to be with Eva in the present, but to go right back to the start of it all, to the days when we had walked in the spring lanes and been thrilled enough with just loving, to the time when I could, perhaps, have still made better choices for our future; it would have made no difference of course, but I still wanted to go back. Yet wish as I might, it was no good. Across the black evening we darted forward, towards Munich and the long road home.

Chapter Seventeen

That was all a couple of years ago now, though sometimes it feels as though decades have passed, and sometimes that barely a month has gone by. I could go on with my story and write about how ill I became after returning from Germany, how I spent a long time recovering while every German word, every familiar smell, was enough to awaken the panic in me. I could explain how I lost contact with Eva, how I eventually, slowly, regained my health and continued at university; how my world was changed, becoming deeper and sadder, and from that, I like to think, more compassionate and more confident.

Yet perhaps it is because I have spent so much time lately considering past days that I find myself caught up once again with the old images—whenever a mention is made of German history I still see Eva's city with all its years of continuation, from the grim bleakness of the medieval world, through the steel and fumes of Victorian times, to the present day and beyond. And sometimes I feel as though a part of me had always been there, watching over the shifting streets for eight centuries, waiting silently for our moment, until we finally came to live it. I suppose that I will never really understand these feelings, or the dizziness that they bring to my brain, being something to do with emotions that I once felt long ago.

And still, on June mornings when heat chokes the air in a haze of memory with all time's desires and fantasies drawn into one, and on balmy evenings when the past is no more than the chink of a glass away, and even when a distant, glimpsed figure echoes backwards through my mind—I think of that painful, surreal summer. I think of the summer and of a dream that was already lost before I tried to save it, of desperate desire that kills all hope, of a girl whom I shall most probably never meet again and the towns and countryside that we travelled in search of a happiness that could not be found.